A BLACK DOG BOOK

DOG WITH A
BONE

Book 1

HAILEY EDWARDS

Copyright Information

No part of this book may be reproduced in any written, electronic, recording, or photocopying without written permission of the publisher or author. The exception would be in the case of brief quotations embodied in the critical articles or reviews and pages where permission is specifically granted by the publisher or author.

Heir of the Dog
© 2014, 2015 by Hailey Edwards All rights reserved.

Edited by Sasha Knight
Cover by Damonza

Interior format by The Killion Group
http://thekilliongroupinc.com

THE BLACK DOG SERIES

CHAPTER ONE

Burnt ozone tingled in my nose. I inhaled deeply, but all I scented was the coming storm. Thunder boomed overhead, rumbling through the ground under my feet. I was still hunched behind a twisted metal sculpture of a giant rooster when the first lukewarm raindrops splattered on my cheeks.

Movement on my right slammed the brakes on my heart. I squinted where I thought I glimpsed a pale blur, but the sun was too far gone and the scrapyard too dark for me to tell what it had been.

My left palm tingled with suppressed energy. My kind of magic wasn't allowed at the marshal academy.

I had to go. Every second I stood here exposed on three sides was an opportunity to get caught. I filled my lungs until they burned then exhaled slowly, hoping for a clue. Nothing.

It's now or never.

Shoving off the rooster's metallic wing, I ran as fast as I could toward the tower at the center of the rusting maze. Even this far away I spotted the white flag plastered against its pole. If I could just reach it, all this ended. Done. Over. If I had that flag, I could go home. If I got there first.

That was a whole lot of *if*s.

"Cadet Thackeray," a low voice rumbled.

My pulse leapt. New plan. Forget the tower. If Shaw had my taste in his mouth, he would not let me reach it. I needed a new hiding spot *now* before he got close enough to use his lure on me. Once I drew in the hot scent of his skin, it was over. I was lost. His heat would snare me, and I would be his.

As if I wasn't already.

After darting past a promising heap, I hesitated until spotting a pair of large red ears sticking up from behind the twisted carcass of what once was a desk. *Mai.* Best friends shared a lot of things, but their hiding place during final exam was not one of them. I left the small fox to her den and kept running.

Sliding around the corner, I left the small-parts section of the yard and headed toward the stacks of crushed vehicles and rusted-out skeletons of construction equipment. I always avoided this section and the prickly sensation it inspired on my nape. Granted, the odds of the stacks falling and crushing me to a half-blooded fae pulp were pretty slim, but I didn't want to be the exception that proved the rule.

Mud splashed up my legs and soaked my sneakers. I paused to scent the wind, gulping a lungful of patchouli-and-bergamot-flavored air. My skin sizzled and my head whirled as I fought the urge to follow that hot fragrance to the even hotter man producing it. *Bastard.* He wasn't playing fair. Incubus lures were too damn tasty, and I was already nursing one hell of a sweet tooth where my instructor was concerned.

With a frustrated growl, I wound through the automotive graveyard until I stumbled past a truck with its cab mostly intact. I crawled over an engine block to reach the door handle and gave it a tug.

Water lubricated its rusty hinges, and it swung open with a soft whine. I crawled inside and sank onto the floorboard.

Five minutes to catch my breath. Then I would make a break for it. The tower wasn't that far. I wasn't the only prey trapped in this corrugated maze, nor was I the easiest mark out there.

I relaxed into the darkness while mentally pinpointing my location and my best exit strategy.

Scratching noises perked my ears. I tensed, ready to bolt, but heard only rain pelting the roof.

Praying I hadn't plopped down into a mouse nest, I held still and turned my thoughts back to the quickest way to reach the tower. It was tall, built like a tree stand. Climbing it would be a piece of—

I heard it again. Claws raked over metal. Louder this time.

Lightning struck as I peered through the driver's side window, outlining a pale, masculine shape. Cruel nails, bone white and razor sharp, traced a rivulet of water down the glass. The handle clicked. I kicked out and jammed my heel down on the stubby door lock. Through the pane, Shaw glowered.

I felt pretty smug until he speared his fingers into the seams and tore the door from its frame.

"You should have run," he said, fingers circling my ankle and jerking me toward him.

I kicked at his fist and yanked on my leg, but he was too strong. He dragged me forward until he could reach my shirt. Gripping my collar, he pulled me upright, off the floorboard and against his chest. He trailed his nose from the shell of my ear down my throat where my neck met my shoulder.

"I did run." I gasped as his scent enveloped me. "You're faster than you look."

Coarse laughter vibrated through his chest into mine. "I can be, when I see something I want."

My smartass reply stuttered and died on my tongue.

"Speechless," he mused, drawing back to peer into my face with eyes gone ravenous.

Tearing my gaze from his, I stared past his broad shoulders at my endgame, at the soaked flag wringing itself on the pole as winds from the summer storm buffeted the tower and ripped at its hem.

I let him think he had won, let him hold me against him until I was free of the truck and could see a clear path for my feet. While hunger turned his eyes opaque, I admit it, I played the damsel card.

Once the toes of my shoes hit dirt, Shaw sank his nails into my hips while searching me for the white handkerchief shoved deep into the rear pocket of my jeans. Once he removed it, I was "dead". Game over. Exam failed. I shot him a regretful look then slammed the heel of my palm into his nose.

Cartilage crunched and blood streamed down his chin. Shock widened his eyes. He groped at his face on reflex, releasing his hold on me. His nails sliced furrows into his cheeks. While he was stunned, I whirled out of his reach and ran for it. I cleared three yards before his enraged roar made me jump.

"Thierry." His voice boomed.

I wish I had said something clever, but I'm pretty sure I squeaked like a mouse with a cat hot on her tail. Incubi as a race were passionate, hotheaded. Shaw as a man was competitive, driven. Talk about your explosive combinations. Attributes that made him a great instructor also made him an apex predator.

And I was feeling hunted.

It was a new experience for me, and I didn't like it much.

Ignoring the snarling on my heels, I pushed until my thighs screamed and my legs were rubber. I ran until the tower was in sight, and I caught a second wind. The growling behind me increased, and so did my speed. Bursting into an open area, I hesitated at the sight of my classmates huddled together.

A slender woman of Japanese descent stood nude under an umbrella covered in plump cardinals. I guess Shaw had found the fox shifter after all. Damn it. Now she would be stuck retaking the exam. The only thing more competitive than a pissy incubus was a kitsune whose 4.0 GPA had just plummeted.

"Move your scrawny ass," Mai screamed at me. "You're the last woman standing."

Our classmates picked up her cries and began cheering for me. I appreciated the support, but the clapping and whistling made it impossible to hear Shaw's approach. Looking wasn't an option. I had to watch my footing or risk tripping. He was downwind, so I couldn't scent him. I was running blind.

Panting through the last dozen yards, I hit the corroded ladder beneath the tower and hauled my body up toward the hatch in the center. My foot slipped off a rung and hit something. I glanced down to find Shaw squinting up at me through one eye. His other was shut tight under a muddy boot print.

Crap. I climbed faster, hands slipping on the wet metal. At the top, I groped for a latch but found nothing. I wedged my shoulder against the side opposite the hinges, took another peek at a slavering Shaw, then rammed the hatch until the lock buckled and the narrow door burst open. I swung inside, bouncing the wood off Shaw's face as he tried to join me. I winced in sympathy. It was a pretty face.

Wood splintered and metal groaned as Shaw ripped the door from its hinges and hurled it away. There were four open slots about two feet high and six feet wide on each side of the tower. The pole was mounted in the center of the roof, so that's where I headed. I slid through one gap, careful of my footing on the slippery tin. Grasping the pole with one hand, I used it to haul myself up the tower's side.

"Not so fast." Shaw wrapped his palm around my ankle.

"Knock it off," I snarled. "You're going to make me fall."

His other hand clutched my upper thigh. "I'll catch you."

"My hero," I grated between clenched teeth.

I tried kicking where his face should be, but he wrestled with my foot until he popped off my shoe. I wriggled until the second shoe joined the first. His fingers dug into the denim of my soaked jeans. My fingers tightened on the slick pole. Using his grip to balance me on the lip of the open window, I flung out my other arm, locking both hands around the pole and hoisting myself higher.

Shaw's hands crept up to my hips, smoothing over my ass in his search for the pocket where my flag was kept. Two inches lower and he would win. I hated losing, so I brought my knee up hard under his jaw and braced that heel in the window, kicking up and launching myself onto the roof.

While Shaw cursed at me and threatened to bend me over his knee—*kinky*—I found my footing.

Standing tall and proud, I snatched the limp flag from its hooks with a whoop. Glancing down at the cheering cadets, I spotted Mai's mile-wide smile and swung my soggy prize over my head with glee.

In hindsight, the victory dance was overkill. One minute I was shaking what my momma gave me. The next I was crashing through the thin roof and toppling over the jagged edge. Shaw tried to catch me. The ground managed the job for him.

Some hero he turned out to be.

CHAPTER TWO

Awareness seeped in and brought its friends Pain and Agony for a visit. I woke with a groan and a burst of sympathy for piñatas everywhere. My eyelids were sticky, my lashes clumped. I succeeded in opening one eye. Mostly. Vision kicked in a second later, or maybe my brain was the slow starter.

I swallowed to wet my throat. "Am I dead?"

Metal scraped over the floor, and the face of an angel floated into soft focus in the vicinity of my feet. His bronzed skin popped against the pallor of the thin bed sheet covering my toes when he gave them a squeeze. Mahogany curls twisted into knots on his head. The roguish glint to his copper eyes was absent. His lush mouth sagged at the corners, his bottom lip chewed ragged by his white teeth.

"No," Shaw drawled from his chair at the foot of my bed, "but not for lack of trying."

I grinned though it hurt. Shaw was a looker even incubused-out. When he was playing human? *Rawr*.

His thumbs slid past the balls of my feet, massaging my arches until a moan eased past my lips.

Shaw tensed at the sound, his hands falling away. The metal legs of his chair scraped again.

Familiar distance spread between us. I closed my eyes so I didn't have to see it. "Where am I?"

"You're in the medical ward," he answered tightly, "on conclave grounds."

I figured I either had to be there or the fae clinic on Myer Lane. Human hospitals were a no-no. Fae were in the closet, and the fastest way to fling open the doors would be to watch one regenerate in a public hospital.

"Here." Shaw cleared his throat. "I almost forgot."

My eyes popped open and zeroed in on the small box in his hands. He must have fished it out of the ever-ready messenger bag of tricks he kept slung across his shoulder at all times.

He leaned over the bedrail so I didn't have to stretch. The wrapping paper I shredded into confetti on my lap, but his clumsy bow I twisted into a ring for my finger. After cursing my way through multiple layers of tape, I opened the box with a gasp.

My gaze swung up to meet his. "Shaw."

His cheeks went ruddy, and he rolled his shoulder, which was his answer to most every situation. I traced the tiny enamel seal inset into a black leather wallet. *Southwestern Conclave Marshal.* "You didn't have to do this." The room went fuzzy at the edges while I blinked back a rush of giddy tears.

He dropped back into his chair. "Look inside."

I flipped it open and sucked in a sharp breath that fizzled into chuckles. Pinned in the center was a plastic sheriff's badge that looked like it had gone missing from a kid's cowboy-themed birthday party.

"Huh." I tapped the center. "They sure don't make these like they used to."

"It's a placeholder," he said solemnly, "to tide you over until graduation. The magistrates are out of town and can't officiate for two weeks."

The full meaning of the gift bypassed the drugs and slammed into me. "I passed?"

His lips quirked at the corners.

I tossed the gift box at his head. "Is that a yes?"

He set his hand back on my toes. "Yes, that's a yes."

"*Yes*." My arm shot up, fist pump thwarted when I tangled my IV line in the strands of a balloon arrangement I hadn't noticed. I swatted at their goofy latex grins until Shaw took pity and wrangled them for me.

He passed me a small white card. "They're from Mable."

I fingered the rectangle of paper, chuckling when I recognized her looping scrawl. "*You lack the sense God gave chickens,*" I read aloud. "*Even they have the sense to know they can't fly. See you soon. Love, Mable.*"

I passed it back to him, and he leaned the card against the weighted base of the arrangement.

"If it makes you feel any better—" he retreated to his chair, "—Mable whacked me with that hot-pink monstrosity of hers for orchestrating your *near-death event*. I heard and saw actual tweeting birds."

I winced. Mable's purse was the neon-pink love child of shag carpeting and a carry-on suitcase as near as I could tell. I leaned back to inspect the bandage on my forearm. "So…what's the damage?"

He ticked off my injuries on his fingertips. "Shattered hip, broken ankles, snapped—"

"Okay, okay, you can stop." I dragged a hand down my face. "Maybe I don't want to know."

"Dr. Row said you'll be tender for a few days," he continued, "but all the bones have mended."

All mended? All that damage healed? I faked like his response hadn't stunned me. My powers had manifested at puberty. I hit the big one-eight last week. Cuts and bruises, yeah, they vanished in minutes, but broken bones?

Picking at the front of my gown, I kept my voice level. "How long have I been here?"

He checked his watch. "Thirty-six hours, give or take."

When he poured me a glass of water over chipped ice and passed it up to me, I figured my voice sounded rougher than I meant it to. I was grateful for the prop to keep my hands occupied. "Thanks."

The doorknob to my room rattled. Two loud knocks followed.

Shaw cracked a smile. "Someone must have locked the door."

"If you wanted to be alone with me," I teased, "all you had to do was ask."

His grin slipped, his bright eyes eclipsed by the white void of his hunger.

I swallowed hard, suddenly nervous about the locked-door situation. "I didn't mean to…"

He pushed to his feet and started pacing the length of the room. "Do you feel up to visitors?"

"I—I guess." I set the water aside and pushed up higher on the bed. "Where are you going?"

Regret thickened his voice. "Out."

Out, the place he went to feed.

Out, the destination always the farthest he could get from me.

CHAPTER THREE

The sound of raised voices brought my head up and reminded me Shaw had asked if I felt up to having company. I wasn't sure I did, now, but he admitted my visitors before leaving.

A short woman swept into the room looking every bit like Mrs. Claus's twin sister gone country. The tips of her magenta cowgirl boots peeked out from under a flowing bohemian skirt made from patchwork bandanas in shades from white to blush to *holy Moses pass me some sunglasses*. A dainty pink bee pendant provided the accent for her white blouse, last year's birthday gift from yours truly.

Mable was a bean-tighe, a gentle spirit bound to a building for the duration of its existence. Her home was the marshal's office. She was also the receptionist there, and the pusher of my papers, which is how we met.

"Oh, Thierry." She dabbed at her eyes with a coordinating hankie. "What have you done now?"

I held up the gift from Shaw. "I made conclave marshal."

"For real?" a familiar voice squealed from the hall.

Mai burst into the room and planted herself at the foot of my bed. Her chestnut hair was pulled into a stringy ponytail, and her academy issued T-shirt was drenched in sweat. She leaned over, swiped the cup of water Shaw had poured me and downed the contents before she noticed me staring at her.

She rattled the ice chips together. "Were you not done with this?"

"I don't know what that man was thinking." Mable came to the bed and poured me a fresh drink in a clean cup before pressing it into my hand. "I'm just amazed that no one else was seriously injured."

"The class voted. The conditions were our choice." I took a sip. "It's not Shaw's fault."

Mable's eyes narrowed.

"It's not *Mr.* Shaw's fault," I corrected.

Mai's snickering earned her a kick in the hip. *Ow.* They weren't kidding about my ankles.

"You could be a vampire and him a stake through your heart, and you would still defend him."

I rolled my eyes at Mai. "Someone has read one too many vampire romance novels."

"I'll forgive that remark this once." She curled her lip. "You do have a head injury after all."

"I do?" I reached up to touch my scalp. "You know what, I don't need the details."

Mable pulled the chair Shaw had occupied to my bedside and sat. "Where is Shaw by the way?"

"He stepped out." I hadn't realized I was still clutching the wallet until something snapped. One of the points from the sheriff badge fell onto my sheet. "I don't expect him back anytime soon."

The topic of Shaw was dropped so hard it made a sound. There was a definite ringing in my ears.

Mable cleared her throat. "Have you spoken to your mother?"

"She doesn't know I got hurt." I exhaled. "Now that it's over, I don't know if I should tell her."

"Surely her number is in your file..." Her voice trailed into silence.

I picked at the broken plastic triangle. "I had her contact information removed."

"*Thierry.*" Mable made it sound like I had drowned a bagful of kittens. "She's your mother."

"Tee doesn't want her mom to worry." Mai stuck up for me. "You know how her mom gets."

I flinched when Mable didn't disagree.

My mom loved me. I never doubted that for a minute. But when her baby girl's thirteenth birthday party morphed into a teenage horror show, it broke some fundamental thing neither of us knew how to fix. So we faked it, pretended I hadn't killed five of my best friends with a touch of my left hand the night my fae magic kindled, acted like she hadn't given up her home, her job, her life to move us from Galveston, Texas to a speck of a town named Wink so the conclave could protect me.

Her fling with my father, Macsen Sullivan, the Black Dog of the Faerie High Court, had left her saddled with a daughter whose gifts terrified her. It wasn't like she could turn to Mac for help, either. He ditched his human lover the instant a second blue line formed on her pregnancy test. At least Mac scrawled the conclave's address on an envelope on his way out the door. *Nice foresight there, Dad.*

Next time, use a condom.

"Here." Mable hefted her bag onto her lap and tugged a package wrapped in festive pink paper from its depths. "This is for you."

Bracing for a pinksplosion, I gingerly unwrapped a white gift box. *So far, so good.* "Wow." I lifted a brown leather messenger bag from its tissue paper bed and traced the delicate swoops and swirls stamped into the flap. "It's beautiful."

She shook a finger at me. "A marshal must be prepared for any situation."

Lifting the bag to my nose, I inhaled the fresh leather scent.

Mable delved into her purse again and presented me with an envelope. "This is also for you." She took my gift and hooked it on the bathroom doorknob.

"What is it?" The conclave seal was printed on the front. So was my name. Very official-like.

"Open it." Mai grabbed for it.

I stopped her with a palm to her forehead. "Get back."

"Girls," Mable sighed.

"She started it," we said together.

Smothering a grin, Mable folded her arms. "Open the letter."

I tore into it, read it once, read it twice and then my jaw dropped. "You're kidding me."

Tiny bubbles of excitement fizzled in my chest until I couldn't breathe.

Mai snatched the paper, leaving me holding the torn corners mashed between my fingertips.

"Marshal Thackeray is to report to Marshal Shaw at the Southwestern Conclave Main Office on Monday at eight a.m. to start on-the-job training." Mai hummed the opening bars of "Don't Stand So Close to Me" by The Police. "That's hot. Six weeks just you, him and a set of restraining Words…"

Heat licked up my neck to sizzle in my cheeks. "This is serious, Mai."

The magistrates would tear a strip off my hide if I got kinky with the spelled Words we used for restraining suspects. Most fae had iron allergies, but their metal sensitivities ran the gamut. Better to detain them with magic now than risk a lawsuit later.

"This is your career," Mable agreed. "I respect Shaw as a marshal. I respect him as an instructor, and I believe his years of experience in the field can help you to become the marshal you want to be. But there are reasons why you two are paired so often..." she hesitated, "...despite concerns about the appropriateness of your relationship raised last year, and you should keep those reasons in mind."

Reasons like he was the only marshal in the state of Texas resistant to my brand of magic, which volunteered him for all things Thierry. There had been talk of bringing in a transfer to alleviate some of the concerns over how much time we spent together, but the whispers never amounted to anything.

I'm sure the shortage of willing victims had nothing to do with it.

My father was the Black Dog, a death omen, like me, and like me he was bound into service to both the Seelie and Unseelie houses. Macsen was a devoted servant of Faerie, a true neutral who bowed to neither house and granted neither the light nor the dark fae exception. He was a renowned hunter who never lost his quarry, an executioner whose mercy could not be bought, begged or borrowed.

His were big shoes to fill. If he had bothered to stick around, I might have tried them on for size.

"I'm not going to mess this up. I can't." Conclave auspices were conditional, after all. They may have solved my legal problems with mortal authorities, but they expected a return on their investment.

I told myself becoming a marshal was my idea, my dream. Most days I even believed it.

"This job means everything to Tee," Mai said. "She won't mess it up, even for a hot piece of—"

"*Mai*," Mable snapped.

Mai dissolved into chuckles, flopping backward across the foot of the bed and crushing my toes.

Yowch.

Mable fanned her face as she stood. "On that note, I believe I will leave you girls to it." Heaving her purse onto her shoulder, she dropped a kiss onto the crown of my head. "See you Monday, dear."

Mai wiggled her fingers but didn't sit up again. Sensing her preoccupation, I waited until Mable left then settled against my pillows and waited for her to speak. When she didn't, I nudged her thigh.

"I'm not cut out for this." She twisted onto her side to face me. "Marshaling is hardcore."

Unsure where this conversation was headed, I shrugged. "I guess."

"Eight cadets were trapped in a scrapyard—can you say tetanus?—with a hulked-out incubus on a white handkerchief killing spree." She widened her chocolate eyes. "Only one made it out alive."

I snorted. "It wasn't that bad."

"Says the girl with the badge on her lap," Mai quipped.

"Yes, five year olds everywhere envy me." I flung the broken corner at her. "What will you do if you drop out?"

"Hayashis and the conclave go way back." She wrinkled her nose. "I'll think of something."

A cold knot congealed in my gut. No more academy meant no more roomie. Mai would have to clear out of our quarters, maybe before I was released. "Does this mean you're moving back home?"

"Are you crazy?" She shoved upright. "I've tasted freedom, and it is sweet. Home is out."

I pushed higher on the bed. "So what are you going to do?"

She leaned forward. "It's what *we're* going to do."

"Okay." I drew out the word. "What are *we* going to do?"

"Get an apartment." She got on her knees and danced until she dragged the cover down my legs. "We're eighteen. You've got your first job, and I've got...parents willing to spot me the rent money."

"I—" I blinked. "An apartment?"

She stopped her one-woman wave long enough to cast me a serious look. "I know you don't like to talk about it, but you and your mom are in a better place now than you have been since we met."

She was right. Mom was downright chipper when I called now that I was out from under her roof.

"Absence, heart, fonder," I said.

"Exactly," she agreed. "So let's do this." She stuck out her hand. "Roomies?"

Feeling lighter than I had in years, I shook on it. "Roomies."

CHAPTER FOUR

Shaw wasn't home anymore. Flames roared over my head, filling my nose with the scent of burnt hair as I crawled on my hands and knees toward him. His shirt hung in singed tatters from one shoulder. He squatted behind an antique chaise lounge with soot tracks blackening the gray upholstery. Blisters covered his neck and torso. Color leached from his skin and hair, his eyes. As I watched, his nails lengthened, sharpened. Hunger stared at me through his whited-out eyes and wet his lips.

Chills swept up my spine while sweat dripped from my hairline into my eyes.

So far my first day of OJT was a hot mess, literally.

While debating whether the danger was greater in staying put or in crawling forward, a blast of heat forced me to roll out of my hiding spot into his. I landed on my stomach, face level with his ass.

It wasn't the worst view I'd had all day.

"What the hell is that?" I yelled, shoving my messenger bag behind my back. This sure wasn't the docile pygmy ouroboros on our paperwork.

Ouroboros were basically self-devouring snakes. Completely harmless even when riled because they were too busy digesting their tails to bother with biting their handlers. This call, my first official one, should have been easy. Bag and tag the little guy then cart him back to the office for processing.

On paper, this wasn't an instance of a fae behaving badly. This was a fae recovery mission. We assumed a human collector had snatched the pygmy, which happens, but that theory had just gone up in smoke. Again, literally.

"I can't get a good look at it," he rumbled.

I patted my head to check for hot spots. "Can you drain it?"

His glare made me flinch.

"Sorry I asked."

Incubi fed on energy. Sex might be their preferred method of feeding, but they could sustain themselves in other ways. The problem being most alternative methods were lethal to mortal prey.

Not that I could judge. I had my own hungers to battle.

I knew for a fact Shaw could feed by absorbing energy through touch, but he had compared the experience to sipping through one of those tiny coffee straws. To quench his thirst, he required a more direct conduit.

In a manner of speaking, I had just asked Shaw to—at best—stick his straw into the bottle of an unidentified fae. At worst I had suggested he boink a flamethrower who might flambé his manly bits.

"Stay down." He pressed his palm to my nape, nails digging into my spine. "I'm going in."

"Wait. I'll go—" I sat up as he leapt the chaise and vanished into the wall of smoke, "—with you."

Thirty seconds passed to the rapid tapping of my toes. I was chewing the inside of my cheek like bubblegum when a bestial roar shook the floor straight up to the rafters. Ceiling beams collapsed into the center of what had been a rancher's home office. At least it had been until whatever was in there hocking up fireballs had turned this end of the house into its lair and the cattle ranch into an all-it-could-eat brisket buffet.

"Shaw," I screamed at the top of my lungs. Between the roaring and the fire, I was almost deaf.

Clenching my left fist, I contained the tingles spreading across my palm, lighting up the runes covering my hand.

This wasn't the academy, this was real life, and this creature had crossed a line.

There were no restrictions placed on magic used in self-defense while in the field.

I smiled.

It was time to earn that badge.

After shoving to my feet, I leapt the smoking chaise and burst through the black cloud making it hard to breathe. I landed in a crouch and opened my senses. My nose might as well have been stuffed with tissue. My eyes watered nonstop. Hissing and spitting made me spin around, but it was just the fire.

I crept forward until my toes hit debris with some give to it. I stepped wide to cross it, but once I had my weight balanced on the other side, a hand grasped my ankle. Startled, I slid and fell on my ass. I reached down and braced myself to stand. My hand brushed over a scrap of fabric. I walked my fingers higher, touched the corner of a metal star then yanked them back, swearing a blue streak.

The cushion from my fall was Shaw. It was his hand clutching my ankle. I bent lower to see if I had a better shot at visibility beneath the smoke. No dice. I resisted the urge to check him for injuries in case my examination hurt him worse. He brought my hand to his lips, which were moving, but the words were lost to the crackle and snap of our surroundings. I had fisted his shirt and was heaving him toward the front door when I was knocked sideways, and my head bounced off a shattered china cabinet's edge.

Freaking monkeys. That hurt. Two head injuries inside of a week. That couldn't be good for me.

Fur brushed past my shoulder. What the hell? I cracked the back of my skull against the cabinet again when a tawny muzzle appeared at the end of my nose. The lips pulled back, exposing sharp teeth and a sandpaper tongue panting from the heat of the building. Charred fur clumped around a leonine face. One of its eyes was an oozing welt. The other it had trained on me while drawing in a series of rapid breaths. Wait. It wasn't panting. *Holy crap.* It was—

I dove aside as it spewed flame where I had been standing.

"A chimera," I yelped. "I'm supposed to extinguish a flipping chimera? Alone? Shaw?"

No help from that quarter. Shaw and his bag of tricks were down for the count. Shoving off the busted frame behind me, I steadied myself while glass sliced into the meat of my palm. Wincing at the sharp bite of pain, I hissed as pulses of magic knit my skin back together.

Peridot light knifed through the hazy air. The chimera narrowed its eye on me, curled its lip and then charged with a bone-rattling roar. I braced myself, shouted a prayer and raised my left hand.

The magic gathered in my palm exploded with the creature on contact. The pulse of energy slammed me backward, locked its teeth into my prey and brought it toppling down on top of me in a twitching heap. I should have stopped. I could have left it alive, but I was hurt. Shaw was...I didn't know...and I was pissed off too.

I fed my runes more and more power, until magic seeped under the chimera's skin and lit it from the inside. I could have stopped then, but I didn't. Jagged bolts of pain shot through me, cramping my lungs and twisting my gut. I was dying. No. I was experiencing its death. Agony zinged through my limbs, but I clung to the chimera, pumping every ounce of juice I had into its muscular body.

While it twitched and jerked, I rolled it off me and crawled to my knees, then onto my feet.

Worse sensations spread over my face and neck, like sunburnt skin cracking. Tears poured down my face, but I couldn't let go now. I had gone too far. My magic sniffed out the chimera's essence. It found the sweetest spot, the still-beating heart. It ripped into that succulent energy, and it feasted.

I was licking my lips when the fur gripped in my fist sloughed off the body and fell to the floor. I was left holding the lush pelt of a lion with a goat's hind legs and a snake's head for a tail that withered to a paper-thin husk as I watched. I looked down at my hand in shock. That had never happened before.

A broad palm wrapped around my upper arm, and I almost jumped out of my skin.

Shaw's eyes shot wide when he recognized the pelt in my hand and the meaty corpse at my feet for what they were. He recovered in the next second and jerked me—and the pelt—through the flaming debris into the yard.

After scanning me from head to toe, he grabbed my shoulders and shook. "What the hell?"

"I don't know." My injuries from last week began screaming at me. "It just happened."

"You skinned him. How did you—?" He seemed to realize he was hurting me and exhaled. "Did you feed?"

Shame tightened my gut. I had to find somewhere else to look.

"That's a yes." He pinched my chin between his thumb and finger and swung my face toward him. "Don't hide this from me."

"I'm not hiding." I stared at a particularly deep crease in his forehead. "I'm just—"

"Look at me when I'm talking to you."

His tone snapped my gaze to his. Shaw's eyes were warm now, copper. All traces of the incubus had been erased, and he looked…almost human.

"I did what you taught me. I fed. I did like we practiced. I reached inside him and I…" my voice trembled, "…don't know. I didn't stop. I was angry. I was hurt and you…" I bit my lip. "I thought…"

He crushed me against his chest. "Don't do that thing where your eyes leak, okay?"

My damp laughter was muffled against his shirt.

"We'll figure this out." His lips moved against my cheek. "You handled yourself in there."

"I was terrified," I admitted, forcing myself out the comfort of his arms.

He cracked a smile that split his lip. "That just means you're smart."

I studied the smoldering heap behind him. "Is it always going to be like this?"

"Nah." Shaw glanced over his shoulder. "We won't always get the good calls."

CHAPTER FIVE

After a brief visit to the medical ward, where Dr. Row's glare flayed what untouched skin I had left, I had another three hours' worth of paperwork standing between me and the cold shower waiting back at my now-empty dorm room.

Paperwork. Hours of it. Sixteen weeks of marshal academy and no one mentioned this?

Clean, tired and lightly coated with balm for my healing blisters, I flopped back on my bed.

My eyes closed, and my day got just a smidge better.

"Thierry," a muffled voice called through the door.

I shot upright so fast I toppled over the twin bed's edge.

"Shaw?"

A pause. "Were you expecting someone else?"

"Not hardly," I groused. "I wasn't expecting you."

My ankles twinged when I put my weight on them. My hip wasn't thrilled with me either. After I flung open the door, Shaw's eyes glinted with mischief. Inwardly cringing, I pasted on a tight grin.

"I respect your love of the classics," he said, brushing past me to enter the room.

Crossing my arms over the vintage Pooh Bear face covering my chest, I glared. "So."

One of his eyebrows lifted. "You're not going to ask me to sit?"

The one chair in the room was buried under a mountain of clean laundry that had spilled onto it from my desk.

I gestured toward his options. "Which bed, Mr. Incubus, would you prefer?"

His mouth opened, but he snapped it shut and kept his smartass response to himself.

"I brought you something." He reached into his back pocket and pulled out an envelope.

Frowning, I crossed to him and accepted the letter. "Have I been reassigned?"

He tapped it. "Open it."

"I know you know what it is." I tore the flap. "Why not answer a simple question for once?"

"A little thing called anticipation," he answered.

I looked inside. Blue paper peeked up at me with numbers almost like a... "Is this a real check?"

His second eyebrow joined the first. "As opposed to a fake one?"

"This is for twenty-five hundred dollars." The room started spinning, so I sat down fast. "Is this a workman's comp thing?" I double- and triple-checked the front. Yes, that really was my name on it.

He chuckled and dropped onto Mai's old bed. "It's your first bonus."

"The ouroboros didn't carry a bounty." I knew. I had checked.

"No, but the chimera did." He dragged a hand over his mouth. "We aren't sure what the connection between them was. Two rare fae breeds don't just materialize on a cattle ranch near Odessa, Texas."

Not without leaving a string of crispy corpses in their wake. "What about the owners?"

"The rancher and his wife—Jake and Bethany Richardson—are both fully human."

Curious at his tone, I tilted my head. "You spoke to them?"

Conclave badges were enchanted. Human or fae, people saw what they expected to see. It was a harmless bit of glamour on our part, something to help us interact with humans without involving the human authorities. Most folks saw marshals as local cops, some figured them for FBI or even MIB.

Until fae came out to humanity on a global scale, marshals had to do the best they could to cover up the supernatural messes fae justice sometimes left behind.

"The man cried when I broke the news his prize Hereford was barbeque." Shaw scrubbed a hand down his face. "His wife, though. She's one of those polished types. Commutes from her high-class digs in Dallas to visit her husband every second weekend and on major holidays. If you ask me, the missus didn't seem that shocked to come home and find her house toastier than a s'more. In fact, after being informed that they both had to stay local, she was more upset at the prospect of spending the night in a hotel with her husband than over the loss of their home."

Interesting. "Are we talking socialite or career woman?"

"She's an interior designer."

"An interior— Wait. How do you know all this?" My breath caught. "Are we investigating?"

His eyes twinkled. "Got the case files in my truck."

Like a struck match, my imagination ignited. My fingers itched to thumb through those papers. I forced the tight lump down my throat. Rookies drew low-priority cases during OJT. That meant most training officers coasted for about six weeks while their temporary partners learned the ropes. Heck, after completing OJT, most marshals remained in the special operations division by choice, acting as glorified bounty hunters for the bonuses alone. That's what Shaw had done, that's what I wanted too.

Inspectors were stretched thin and shared across all divisions. They tended to burn out faster and either quit or drift back to spec ops.

Taking on this case, in that role, stamped a gold star on my resume.

"Do you need a moment?" His lips spread in a grin.

I shook my head, thoughts whirling. "Is the missus initiated?"

The number of initiated humans kept climbing every year as fae interbred with humans, but they were generally a tight-lipped community, given the fae they knew were their loved ones. In cases where blood wasn't a good enough reason to protect fae secrets, a visit from a friendly, neighborhood marshal generally was.

"As far as we can tell," he said, "she has no fae relatives or reason to know of our existence."

"Can we access her client list?" I worried my lip. "Find out if any of her clients are initiated?"

He gave me a thoughtful look. "What are you thinking?"

"That it's a tough economy. You've got to have serious connections with deep pockets to keep a business like hers in the black. Her husband's might have proven too shallow. It took a lot of cash to float a ranch that size too." I mulled over the remains of the fire. "Any evidence on site is toast."

Shaw made a sound that was neither agreement nor disagreement. I had missed something.

Rare fae. Humans. Greed. "At what temperature does iron melt?"

The tiny crinkles at the edges of his eyes told me he was pleased with the direction of my thoughts.

"Twenty-seven thousand and fifty degrees Fahrenheit," he answered without hesitation. "Before you ask, the average house fire burns between nine hundred and eleven thousand degrees Fahrenheit. Even if you factor in the chimera's breath that started it, it still won't reach smelting temperatures."

That was good news. "Were any cowbells found inside the house?"

"None in the reports I've seen." When I deflated, he added, "They're still sifting through ash. If any were recovered, it's possible they haven't been recorded yet." He paused. "I hate stating the obvious, but it's a working ranch. Cowbells can be explained away ten different ways from Sunday."

"That doesn't mean they aren't belling," I argued. "They just haven't been caught."

The term belling originated from the practice of hanging cowbells on leather collars around the creatures' necks. Most fae suffered iron allergies, and most vintage cowbells were iron cast. Prolonged contact with the bell poisoned the fae. Bury a corpse intact and the iron, over a period of years, dissolved the flesh and bones, leaving no evidence of a crime.

Why bells? Early poachers chose an item that naturally went missing from farmers' livestock and whose absence raised no one's suspicions. Shocker, poachers were all-around thieves. They even pilfered their poaching supplies. If a farmer got pissed about it, then local boys would be found with stolen bells in their possession. The incident would be excused as a prank, the boys punished and the poachers given time to relocate their operation.

Through the years, later generations of poaching sickos kept the grisly tradition alive.

He held my gaze and waited. "I'm not disagreeing with you."

Poaching rare animals from the fae realm was a capital offense. If you stole a treasure from Faerie, you paid for it with your life. No givebacks, no exceptions.

I chewed on my thumbnail. "What about the husband?"

"Lives on the ranch, handles the day-to-day operations." Shaw's lips pursed as he dredged through his memory. "Likes four-wheeling and hunting, as most good ol' Southern boys do. He spent a small fortune on a storm shelter installation a few years back. After watching a grown man cry over a cow named Richardson's Buck Ton Son of a Gun, I'm wondering if he didn't build it big enough to accommodate his cattle too."

"Stranger things have happened." People could get downright weird about their animals. "Maybe we should forget the ranch and focus elsewhere."

"By elsewhere," Shaw said, "I assume you mean Dallas."

I gave a slow nod. "The bigger the city, the dirtier its underbelly."

He scratched his cheek. "I haven't handled one of these cases in a while."

Thanks to his stint as an instructor for yours truly. "If you're not up to it…"

"We'll leave tomorrow afternoon." His eyes glinted. "I'll book the hotel."

"Separate rooms," I blurted.

"I was thinking separate beds."

I mentally stumbled. "I snore."

"I know." His gaze swept over me. "We've slept together before."

Chimera-grade heat blasted into my cheeks. "There were nine other people there."

His shoulder lifted. "Their tents weren't next to mine."

"You were the one who assigned lots," I spluttered. Granted, there had been conclave-sanctioned restrictions on how far apart we got due to the nature of my talent and concerns for my fellow cadets' safety, but still.

His features settled into an innocent expression. "I thought a rogue bear broke camp perimeter."

I returned the favor. "Do you often run out of tents naked to confront danger?"

He didn't blink. "Commando is more comfortable for me."

"What about the rest of us? Nine other people saw your twig and berries."

He shifted closer to the edge of the bed. "Twig?"

I struggled to keep my face neutral. "As in small stick?"

He huffed. "This is an inappropriate conversation to be having with—"

"I'm not a minor or a child or whatever other diminutive noun you were about to spew."

"I was going to say my partner."

"Oh."

"I should let you get some rest." He stood with a frown. "I didn't ask. How are you feeling?"

"The energy from the chimera patched me up pretty well. I've got no complaints. You?"

His gaze drifted to the floor. "Same here."

That explained a few things. Between the surprise of finding him on my doorstep and the shock of what he brought with him, I hadn't absorbed the fact that he was mostly healed. A fair amount of light bruising remained, but the dark smudges would fade after he caught an hour or two of good sleep.

I saluted him with the envelope still held tight in my grip. "Thanks for bringing me the check."

"No problem." He lifted his hand, gaze pinned to the wall behind my head. "Night."

"Night."

He opened the door, hesitating on the threshold. "What you asked earlier."

We had covered so much ground, he could have meant anything. "Yeah?"

"My answer is whichever one you're in." He slammed his palm into the casing then left.

I sat there, mind whirling. What had I asked? What had I said? What did he mean? Spearing my fingers through my hair, I tugged on the roots. As tired as I was, my brain was soup. I couldn't think without it leaking out my ears.

I gave up and stomped to the bathroom, snatching my cell off the counter. I punched redial.

"Tee?" Mai sounded panicked. "You didn't fall in the shower, did you?"

"Yes, Mai. I also showered with my phone in hand, just in case."

"That's not funny, Little Miss Head Injury."

"I'm sorry." I ground my palm into my eye. "I'm just tired and grumpy."

"Is that why you called? Should I sing you a lullaby or read to you from Wiki?"

"Um, no. Thanks, but no thanks." I wandered back to bed and lifted the check. "You know how I said it would take some time for me to save up my half of the deposit on an apartment and the utilities?"

"Yes, and I totally understand. No pressure. I can deal with moving home as long as I know it's temporary." She paused. "That's not why you're calling, is it? This is temporary, right? Thierry?"

"I got paid my first bonus today."

"Wow. On your first day?" She exhaled on a whistle. "Go you."

"It's for twenty-five hundred dollars."

"Damn."

"Do you still have that list of apartments for lease on the fae side of town?"

"Yeah, they're in my purse."

"Good. I'll pick you up at eight. We'll take some tours and maybe sign some papers, okay?"

Her earsplitting squeal made me flinch.

"I'm hanging up now," I yelled into the receiver.

She was still going strong when I hit the end button.

Crawling into the empty bed in my lonely room, I set the alarm and flipped off the lights.

Once my aching head hit the pillow, I remembered.

"...which bed do you prefer?"
"...whichever you're in."

CHAPTER SIX

With the Dallas trip looming, I got a pass on clocking in at the office in favor of packing. Since I lived in jeans, sneakers and the faded T-shirts of boyfriends past, that took me all of twenty minutes.

Besides the bonuses for high-risk captures, my favorite job perk had to be the casual dress code.

After inhaling a raisin bagel, I dialed up a fae taxi service to drive me to the fae section of town. I was still picking at the blister bubbles on the heels of my favorite sneakers when the cabbie slammed on his brakes.

"This it?" His eyes met mine in the rearview mirror. His were yellow, his pupils elliptical.

Hey, I'm not saying the guy was a feline, but those eyes and that tone coaxed a growl out of me.

"Down, girl." He flashed a mouthful of needlelike teeth.

Yep. Definitely a cat.

My gaze slid over the familiar McMansion the Hayashi family called home. "This is me."

"You sure you're not lost?" he pressed.

Ready for some fresh air, I gripped the door handle. "I'm good, but thanks."

"I'm only checking 'cause you smell familiar, and I don't want no trouble." He drummed stubby fingers on the steering wheel. "If you light this place up, I don't want no trail leading nobody back to me."

"Light it up?" My palms went damp. "Who do I remind you of?"

"Macsen Sullivan." He twisted to face me. "The spitting image. You related or something?"

"Or something." I resisted the urge to flash my palm and ask how it compared to the original.

Two types of fae knew my father, those he worked with and those he brought down.

I learned early not to ask questions about Mac. No one, not even my mother, answered them.

The cabbie's eyes cut left, and a purr rumbled in his chest. "Foxy lady. She a friend of yours?"

Through the glass I spotted Mai jogging down the drive to meet me. She wrestled two squirming kits in her arms, red furballs whose playful nips made her wince. I noticed the cat still staring. "Roll that sandpaper tongue back into your mouth." I tossed a few bills into the front seat then stepped out.

He lowered the nearest window, whistled at Mai, then peeled out before I became a stereotype—I was not going to chase after that car to give him a piece of my mind.

Mai ignored the kit gnawing on her hair. "Did you forget to tip him or what?"

"Cat," I said by way of explanation. "Who are those little cuties?"

"Margo and Fargo." She rolled her eyes. "They're my newest niece and nephew."

"Twins?"

She snorted. "Does a fox have a tail?" The friskier of the two kits clamped onto her earlobe. Mai yelped, gripped its scruff and tugged, then held it at arm's length. "We don't draw blood on family."

"Are you babysitting?" I pulled out my phone. "Is this a bad time? I can call for a pick-up. I'm sure Kitty McLitterbox would love to come back for me."

"If you leave me," she snarled, "I will hunt you down, chop you up and feed you to Grandmother's koi."

I believed her. "Are all kitsunes this violent, or are you the exception?"

She glanced toward the house. "You've met my mother and grandmother."

"Good point."

She hooked a thumb over her shoulder. "Do you want to come in?"

I waved her on. "I'll wait here." The better not to become fish kibble for her grandmother's scaly BFFs.

Mai huffed bangs out of her eyes but swallowed her lecture on how I needed to be socialized.

Once she turned her back, I indulged in a balance exercise and walked the curb. A misstep—stupid ankle—sent me stumbling into the grass. It was softer than the curb, so I sat and let my eyes go out of focus. The houses began fading, the road crumbled. The scent of fresh-cut grass in the air turned to dust in my lungs. As I sifted through the complex layers of glamour hiding this part of town from human eyes, the tidy subdivision faded from sight into a long dirt road going nowhere.

A door slammed shut behind me, snapping me from my thoughts.

"I assume we're taking my car," Mai called.

I blinked free of the camouflage, and the outlines of houses rushed back into clear focus. "Against my better judgment."

"Good. No offense." She pushed a button on her key fob, and the garage door opened. "But your mom's car is on its last leg—wheel? She should put it out of its misery. It would be a mercy killing, seriously."

"It's not that bad." Mom's sedan was older than I was, but it had lasted this long. Parts of it anyway.

With a shake of her head, Mai slid behind the wheel of her celery-green coupe, a graduation gift of the nonreturnable kind, stomped on the gas and spun wide, almost sideswiping me in the process.

My knees were still knocking from my near-death experience when she lowered a window.

Patting the tiny bucket seat beside her, she called, "Hop in."

I opened the door, folded myself inside and grasped the seat belt. Groping under my hip, I finally located the receptacle and rung the slot. She spun out before I took my right foot off the ground.

"Sorry," she chimed. "You said we're in a hurry, right?"

I nodded, compressing my lips while fighting to keep down my breakfast.

"Does it strike you as odd that two days into your OJT, Shaw found a way to whisk you away to a fancy-schmancy hotel for a night?" she mused. "In Dallas? Far away from prying conclave eyes?"

The next turn had me swallowing hard. "It was my idea," I muttered from between tight lips.

She cut her eyes my way, which did terrible things to my blood pressure. "Nice."

"Nothing is going to happen."

She clicked her tongue. "Not with that attitude."

"He's my partner."

She waved one of her hands. "Before that he was a friend and then he was your instructor."

Wrong. Shaw had never been my friend. He had been the super-hot guy the conclave called in to chaperone the field trips I went on with other fae children when Mom flaked on me at the last minute.

"I don't get the resistance," she grumbled. "You're a Class R fae—a freaking Rarity, babe. That means you can have any guy you want, and the conclave can't say boo about it. Under the Bylaws of Earthen Cohabitation, any rare fae born on Earth is granted unrestricted access to the mate or—" she wiggled her eyebrows, "—*mates* of their choice. If you want Shaw, you can have him. No red tape."

"The last thing I need is to be *that* girl." I huffed. "Entitlement looks good on exactly no one."

"Yeah, yeah." Her eyes took on a dreamy quality. "But don't you wonder what it would be like?"

Every time I look at him. "This trip is for work."

"Playing is more fun," she chirped in a singsong voice.

"So says the fox." I snorted. "Speaking of work, have you decided on your next move?"

"I'm glad you asked." She sat up straighter. "I've spent so much time talking you off ledges that the perfect job just popped into my mind." She patted the accelerator. "I'm going to be a counselor."

How to respond to the announcement my screwed-up childhood inspired my best friend's calling? "Wow."

"Fae youth are struggling more now than ever to adapt to the duality of their existence."

I did a double take. "Someone spent quality time with Google last night."

"You laugh, but this is serious. On one hand, we tell children to embrace their fae heritage. On the other, we teach them to be secretive and mistrustful. Some fae are so deep in the closet their kids don't know they are fae." She cast me a sharp look. "I don't have to tell you how dangerous that is."

"This new career path sounds great," I groused, "but could we make this not about me?"

"If it makes you feel any better, as a conclave employee, all our future conversations will be considered privileged information." Mai slid her eyes off the road long enough to wink at me. "So if you want to have a chat about what happens between you and Shaw tonight, it will go no further than my nonexistent office."

I rolled my eyes.

"I didn't notice before." Her brow puckered. "You look different. Is saying you look radiant too cliché?"

Pretending interest in the view, I shifted so I could rest my elbow on the door. "I fed yesterday."

Mai took one hand off the wheel, which almost gave me a coronary, and put it on my thigh. She didn't speak. She understood what it meant to me, how much I hated that part of myself. Honestly, I think that's why she shipped me and Shaw so hard. Even if I hadn't been nursing a crush on him for years, she saw the commonalities, but I wasn't as sure that two soul-suckers could be soul mates.

His hunger wanted me all right. Maybe more than the man himself did.

CHAPTER SEVEN

Several hours and apartment tours later, I greeted Shaw with a spring in my step.

"What's with that smile?" He leaned against the passenger-side door of his rental car.

I rolled my suitcase around to the rear bumper and fished a set of keys from my pocket. "Ta-da."

"Nice." He popped the trunk and added my luggage to his. "What do they go to?"

"An apartment in Rolling Hills." I jingled them. Music to my ears.

He laughed until I put them away. "I guess I don't have to ask where your bonus went."

"Nope." I rounded the car. "Now I'm financially back to square one. So this trip better pay off."

Shaw jogged to get ahead of me, opening my car door like the gentleman I was sure he wasn't. I used the moment of silence while he circled to his door to pull on my game face. He seemed like the same old Shaw to me. What he meant or didn't mean last night was in the past. *Forget it. Move on.*

When Shaw slid into the car, a faint whiff of earthy patchouli followed him.

I tried very hard not to wonder where he had come from just now. It made sense for him to fuel up before taking a long trip into the city. I wish I hadn't known anything about it.

"Check under your seat." He strapped in, skimmed his gaze over me to make sure I was settled, then merged into the light evening traffic.

I groped the floorboard until my fingers bumped a stiff edge. I was guessing a manila folder. After scooping it up, I cracked the thick file open across my lap and began skimming the front page.

"That's everything we could find on the Richardsons. Maybe you'll see something I missed."

"I doubt that," I murmured. I caught his pleased smile from the corner of my eye. Guys were so easy.

His fingers drummed the wheel. "You've got six hours to mull it over before we reach Dallas."

My back ached thinking about it. "Explain again why we couldn't fly?"

"On a scale of one to five," he said with a dollop of sarcasm, "you and I are threat level fours."

"That's bogus." I huffed. "We're marshals. We're the good guys."

"We're also predatory species who could do a lot of damage to the few hundred humans trapped with us in a tin can in the sky." He sounded resigned. "It sucks for our kind, but them's the breaks."

I didn't correct him. I didn't have a kind. Like Mai said, Mac was unique. That made me one of a kind too.

"Huh." I shifted my attention to the Richardson file. "Bethany was born in Hastings, Nebraska." I grabbed my phone and accessed a map. "What are the odds that Hastings is spitting distance from Lebanon, Kansas?"

"It's an hour drive," he said without hesitation. "Spitting distance is out unless she's part llama."

Oh ha-ha. I hadn't expected the location to be breaking news. He would have spotted the nearness to the conclave's U.S. headquarters right off the bat.

"The missus is what—mid-forties?" I pocketed my cell then flipped to her picture and bio. "A very well-preserved forty-six."

"You're reaching," he cautioned.

"There were riots in Lebanon during the mid-seventies when the first wave of trolls was granted the right to use the tether between realms to cross into the mortal realm and make their home here."

"That's circumstantial evidence at best," he cautioned. "The conclave crushed the riots and spun the news coverage so humans thought a religious cult had imploded. Bethany was seven. I doubt she showed any undue interest in the news at that age. Nice catch, but you have to dig deeper."

I arched an eyebrow.

Chuckles rumbled from his throat. "No offense meant."

"None taken." I smiled up at him. "I wouldn't want to bark up the wrong tree."

"I see what you did there," he said dryly.

I smirked into the folder. "It's okay when I do it."

"Of course it is," he said in his *I know better than to argue with a woman* voice.

High on smugness, I sank into reading the file, devouring the typed pages before asking Shaw to help me decipher some of his handwritten notes. By the time we reached Dallas and checked into our hotel room, yes, as in singular, I was exhausted. I was also an expert on one Bethany Marie Richardson.

CHAPTER EIGHT

Normally, I'm the opposite of a morning person. In fact, I have been known to growl at them on principle. Waking up to find Shaw standing half naked in the doorway to our bathroom with only his towel wrapped around his hips perked me up faster than an injection of double espresso to the heart.

I peeked at him from under my lashes, watching as he paced while brushing his teeth. His phone occupied his other hand. Furrows in his brow deepened the faster his thumb stroked the screen.

Shaw stopped with his back to me, giving me time to admire all the hard muscle packed onto his tall frame. Water pooled in my mouth. I wiped the back of my hand over my lips and faked a yawn.

He glanced over his shoulder. "Morning, sleepyhead."

I checked the alarm clock and groaned. "It's six o'clock."

He crossed to the bathroom, spat and rinsed while I was trying to convince my bladder we could roll over and go back to sleep without me having to climb out of a comfy bed to make a pit stop first.

"The magistrates' office emailed." He raised his voice over the running faucet while he prepped to shave, which made my bladder situation worse. "The Richardsons have given their statements and been cleared to leave Odessa, provided they agree to make themselves available for future inquiries."

I pushed upright and swung my legs over the edge of the bed. "What does that mean for us?"

His gaze traveled from my sparkly coral toenails up my calves to my knees. "What?"

Flipping the sheet over my lap, I tried again. "What does that mean for us?"

He killed the faucet. "I couldn't hear over the water." After giving that lie a moment to stink up the room, he pulled the door almost closed. "They can drive the twenty minutes to Midland, catch a ten o'clock flight and touch down at the Dallas/Fort Worth Airport at a quarter after eleven."

"Can we get a confirmation from the marshals in Odessa?" I wondered.

"Already made the call," he yelled. "They'll ring us if/when the Richardsons hop a plane."

I nibbled my bottom lip. The ranch was swarming with marshals. I couldn't think of one good reason for them to go back there. Escape to Mrs. Richardson's second home was their best bet. Or at least hers.

Now that they had been cut loose in Odessa, the marshals could watch them and let us know which way they ran.

"We've got five hours." I tossed the cover aside and shoved into the bathroom with him. "Sorry, but you're the one who wanted to share." Pushing him over the threshold, I slammed the door closed on his heels. Pounding on the door caught me with my sleep shirt halfway over my head. "What was that?" I cranked up the hot water until the shower became a dull roar and grinned evilly. "I can't hear over the water."

My pulse sprinted as I ducked under the steam. Not even a sneak peek of Shaw's abs had given me this sort of rush. A shiver wracked me. I was in serious danger of falling in love with my job.

Mrs. Richardson's apartment was located on the eighteenth floor of a skyscraper in downtown. A man with nondescript features wearing a sedate gray uniform held the door open for us on the street. I was mildly surprised he let us pass until I caught a whiff of spice on the air. The scent tightened my gut, but it also kept the doorman smiling. When the uniformed man behind a desk in the lobby noticed us, he jumped from his chair and chased us to the bank of elevators. Shaw dialed up his lure, hooking the poor guy so hard he shuffled back to his seat with a dopey grin on his face. He was waving his pinky at us as the elevator doors closed.

"Don't say it," Shaw muttered under his breath.

I fanned the residual fragrance away from my face. "Say what?"

He leaned against the wall, letting his head hit it with a thump. "Whatever it is you're thinking."

"Other than hoping we don't plummet to our deaths in a freak accident, my mind is blank."

"That's comforting." He straightened as a chime indicated we had reached our floor. "Ready?"

I gripped my satchel's strap. "Yep."

We had exited the lift together and paused to gain our bearings when it hit me. A sickly sweet scent.

Decay. "There's a body." I inhaled again. "Definitely fae. Recent too. Coming from this way."

I put my nose to use and followed the pungent aroma to apartment three-twenty-two.

"That's the Richardsons' apartment," Shaw confirmed. "Stand back."

He dug in his pocket until he produced a weathered brass skeleton key.

It had a vaguely familiar look, like I had seen one in a picture once. "Where did you get that?"

His smugness level shot off the charts. "From a certain bean-tighe who no longer needed her all-key."

"That's Mable's all-key?" Each bean-tighe was sent out in the world with one. A key that could open any door. So when they found their true home, they could enter without violating the building.

Shaw focused on the lock. "I can neither confirm nor deny that."

"I thought it was a one-time-use deal?"

"It is, for them." He lined the bulky key up to the sleek lock. "I'm not a bean-tighe. The key will work for me until I vow to remain inside the four walls of a building for life, which ain't happening."

"I'll be sure to add one of those to my Christmas list."

"Aren't you a little old to believe in Santa Claus?"

"Have you seen Mable?"

"Point taken."

Hovering at Shaw's shoulder, I watched him press his elongated key into the slit on the knob. It shouldn't have fit. Metal should have hit metal and called it a day. Instead, the lock gaped like one of those cartoon mouths and devoured the key. Shaw turned it, opened the door and then stood there for a good thirty seconds uttering threats involving hammers at the doorknob if it didn't return his key.

Ptui. The lock spat out the key and its thin lips puckered into its previous shape.

"This is all very *Alice in Wonderland.*" I trailed him into the white-on-white living space. "Well, if she skinned the White Rabbit for her couch." There were matching ivory chairs too. "I guess those were his cousins?"

Shaw locked the door behind us. "According to their website, all one-bedroom floor plans have a home office or office nook."

"You take the office." I sniffed out the foul scent trail. "I'll take the bedroom and work my way out."

"Wear these." He tossed me latex gloves. "We don't know what we're dealing with here."

I snapped them on, and the cool tingles of an activated spell swept over my hands.

A king-size bed sat catty-corner opposite me. The bedroom was painted white, but the comforter was crimson. Small black velvet bird appliques swarmed in the center. I'm not much for art. I'll confess the deeper meaning of the twisted comforter was lost on me. Maybe *death to all swallows?*

Speaking of death... The faint essence of decay lingering in the hall shrouded this room. It smelled ground into the accent rugs, and no amount of plug-in air freshener could mask it from a nose as keen as mine. I followed the sharpest whiff of odor straight to the bed and ripped back the covers. The center of the bed, where the sheets should have been white, was a rusty-brown color and crusted with dried blood.

"Shaw," I called.

He padded down the hall, stopping when his shoulder brushed mine. "Is this what you smelled?"

Easing around the side of the bed, I lowered my face six inches above the mattress and inhaled. I straightened slowly, processing the puzzling information. "No. It's not. Someone—or something—else was in here." I gestured toward the stains. "This is old, faint. Human. What I smelled in the hall, and in here, it's hard to describe. The stench has seeped into the walls from constant contact with whatever it is."

His gaze bounced from the en suite bathroom to the closet. "Do you think it's still here?"

"Unless it's hiding in the walls..." which, I'll admit, was a possibility with fae, "...no."

"Then keep searching." He cleared the bathroom and closet. "We'll set a perimeter spell when we leave. I want to monitor the foot traffic in and out of this place for the next forty-eight hours." His gaze swept around the room. "Call if you find anything else."

"Will do." I tugged the mattress off the box spring then stood it against the wall. Stains covered the base and, when I shuffled it aside, more blood had congealed in a puddle on the hardwood floor.

I read once the human body contained five and a half liters of blood.

I bet every ounce of it had spilled here.

Nothing worth noting in or under the bedframe. I kicked aside the crimson area rug and examined the contents of Mrs. Richardson's closet. More shoes than a Payless, but no secret compartments, odd stains or odors.

The bathroom proved less interesting. Jars and tubes filled each drawer, the labels all printed in

French. I collected a few hairs from her brush and bagged her razor. Her nail clippers also got tagged. Nothing unusual so far. Okay, so the freaky stuff only happened in the bed. Didn't it always?

Reentering the bedroom, I noticed two things. The box spring sat on the bedframe as though I had never moved it, and the mattress no longer leaned against the wall but now stood in front of the door.

A blast of cold air shot down my neck, stirring the ripe scent of rot around the room. This was it, the stench from the hallway. I turned a slow circle, coughing as the stench worsened. "Shaw?"

No response.

Okay then.

Keeping it casual, I walked to the mattress and gripped the fabric handles sewn into the sides. It wouldn't budge. I jerked harder. No dice. I threw my weight into tugging it aside when pain stung my hand. I stumbled back, dripping blood from a nasty bite mark swelling across the top of my hand.

So much for the cut-resistant gloves.

A bite like this should have healed a second after the teeth let go, but it wasn't mending. It was festering as I watched. *Ick.*

"Come out with your hands up," I snapped.

Gray mist drifted from behind the mattress and settled across the floor. As the smoke-like twists uncurled, a slender creature no more than two feet high at the shoulder solidified with massive teeth on display. It wore a tailored crimson half vest trimmed with white fur. Factor in the pointy ears and it reminded me of an elf. Not North Pole stock, either. More like Krampus's child-whipping helpers.

Huh. Maybe Shaw was on to something with the Christmas-fascination thing.

"I will do no such thing." The creature straightened his vest. "This is my home."

Uh-oh. House spirits were crazy territorial and—all-key or no all-key—we had trespassed. "What are you?"

"A boggart." He sniffed. "I hope that wet-dog scent washes out."

My jaw clenched. "Listen here, buddy—"

"I am not your *buddy*." He flicked his wrist, and mist crawled across the ground and slithered up my torso. It trapped my legs and clutched my shoulders. Another flick and his rancid fog slung me across the room. My head bounced off the wall. "I must ask you to leave before the mistress arrives."

I pushed upright, wincing as I put weight on my sore hand. "Mistress?"

A boggart could infest a house and terrorize the owners like this one was gunning for me, creating what humans considered a haunting. But the one word said it all, didn't it? *Mistress*. She owned him.

So much for the Richardsons being uninitiated.

The spirit pinched his lips together.

I braced on the wall until I got my feet under me. "We haven't been formally introduced." I showed him my left palm, let him wonder at the soft light pooling on the glossy oak floorboards between us as I gathered power in my hand. "I'm Marshal Thackeray with the Southwestern Conclave's Special Operations Division." His hands went to his vest, smoothing the fabric while he ignored me. "Your mistress is under investigation for poaching." I tagged the bloody bed with my gaze. "And the list is growing."

Hammering at the bedroom door sent relief coursing through me. My hand was a last resort. My power didn't come with an off switch. Every time magic pulsed through my runes, it meant kill or be killed. Right now I was lit up, glowing, and I wasn't sure I could diffuse the energy without feeding.

"Thierry," Shaw called. "Are you all right in there?"

"I'm fine." I jerked my head at the boggart. "Step away from the door so my partner can enter."

"What is that smell? Dirt and oranges?" The spirit sniffed. "What is he?"

Species was up to Shaw to disclose or not. "A conclave marshal, just like me."

Beady eyes darted to my hand then to the air vent overhead. "That is not an answer."

I snorted. "And here you've been so forthcoming."

The boggart straightened his shoulders. "I will speak to you only with my mistress present."

Great, he had just pulled the boggart equivalent of asking for a lawyer. Before I could bluff him into a corner, he turned to vapor and drifted into the vent. At least the stink dissipated once the twerp went airborne.

"The door's locked." The wood muffled Shaw's voice. "Do I need to open it or can you?"

"Give me a minute." I shouldered aside the mattress and twisted the lock with my right hand. "I was just wrapping up an interview with the help." When he glanced around the empty room, I said, "Mrs. Richardson enslaved a boggart."

He brushed past me on his way inside the bedroom. "So the Richardsons are initiated after all."

"Bethany is at least. With their separate living situation, I'm not sure how much the husband knows about what his wife is up to." I circled him. "Also? We have a tiny problem."

He frowned at my hand, at the shine encasing it. "Turn it off."

"You know it's not that easy." I flexed my fingers. "It's all charged up with nowhere to go."

"No one said it was easy. Learning to use my lure was a pain in the ass, but I did it and you will too." He stepped closer. "Slow your breathing. Shake off the residual energy. Release it into the air."

I shut my eyes, focused on each inhale and exhale. Power fizzled in my palm.

"That's it," he soothed. "Relax. Let it go."

His nearness, the soft rumble of his voice, distracted me.

"I can't." Magical residue clung to my skin, softly lighting my runes. "It won't release."

"Do you want me to help?" His voice lowered.

I was afraid to open my eyes as I breathed, "Yes."

His coarse, thick fingers threaded with those on my left hand. My eyes popped open on a gasp when Shaw's lips brushed mine. His taste was warmth and comfort, and it lulled me deeper into his embrace. I was floating when the first tugs registered. My palm stung, the skin burning. From the corner of my eye, I watched as my runes flared brighter before another long draw through my hand extinguished the light. I broke away from Shaw.

His eyes were cloudy. The hand that had held mine was sharp from the growth of his nails.

"Thanks," I rasped.

"Any time," he answered, voice as ruined as mine. He turned to go.

"You didn't have to kiss me." He could have stopped when our hands joined.

"I know."

"Well." I cleared my throat and followed him into the hall. "Okay then."

CHAPTER NINE

Shaw kept his eyes glued to the digital display as it counted down the floors we whooshed past on our way back to the lobby. I bit my lip to keep quiet. No sense in risking the fallout from what I had to say to him if the booth was wired for sound. They hadn't bothered hiding the cameras. They hung in corners, watching silently.

By the time we hit the street, I had worked up a good head of steam. "Why did we leave?"

He kept walking, his long legs outpacing me. "We gathered all the information we could."

"How can you say that?" I grabbed his arm. "Their boggart is a—"

"—slave who would die before incriminating its mistress. It's part of their compulsion. They hate humans, hate fae too, but they're trapped by their nature…" he exhaled, "…just like the rest of us."

I recoiled, a wave of nausea bubbling in my stomach. "I guess that explains the kiss."

He stopped so suddenly I smacked into his back.

"I wanted the kiss." Shaw backed me against a wall of glass, the front of a coffee shop, I think. His palm slapped the pane over my head, pinning me with his body as much as the fury simmering in his dark copper eyes. "Hunger does not control me."

"That was a cheap shot." I rested my hand on his chest. "I shouldn't have taken it."

"Your aim is too good sometimes." He covered my hand with his and gently removed it. He let me straighten, lowered his hand and got himself under control. "If the Richardsons left any evidence behind, the boggart would have hidden it in his den until they returned. By law we can't question an indentured house spirit without its masters present, otherwise their testimony is coerced at best."

"They killed someone there," I reminded him.

"They killed a human." He turned to leave. "That's a matter for the human authorities."

I darted around in front of him. "The Richardsons are human."

He sidestepped me. "They're suspected of committing crimes against Faerie."

A cold realization settled in my chest. "You don't care about them, do you?"

Pinching the bridge of his nose, Shaw regrouped. "I was raised to view humans as food. I might enjoy their company, I might have been fond of a few in my time, but at the end of the day they are a breed apart. They're safer as far from our world as they can get. Don't act like you don't know this."

"If Mac had stuck around," I snarled, "Mom would have been fine in our world."

"You know half their story." He touched my cheek. "Don't judge your father too harshly before you hear his side. Your mother did the best she could by you. She loves you. Your father might too."

I scoffed. "He loves me so much he ditched both of us, so much I've never met him."

"He's old. He was born in Faerie and has lived among the fae most of his life. You can't judge him by human standards. If you do, he'll fall short every time." Shaw started walking, slower this time so keeping up was easier. "I'll make a note on the file, okay?"

"If the Richardsons are proven guilty, they aren't walking away from this." I said it out loud to make it real.

"No, they won't." He took my arm and crossed the road.

I glanced at where his hand gripped me. "You're humoring me."

"Yes." He scanned the stores lining the street. "Your fondness for humans is dangerous."

"Seeing as how I am half *human*," I emphasized, "I do have a vested interest in that part of my heritage as well."

His exhale closed the subject.

A footnote in a report was all dead humans would ever be to most fae. Either I accepted that mortal lives were worth less and turned a blind eye or I bided my time. My partner was temporary. After OJT I could work solo, and I would never let a case with fae-on-human violence get swept under the rug. I owed humans that much. They deserved an advocate. One who wouldn't tolerate this footnote bullcrap.

All of a sudden, I was invested. This wasn't just work, it was an actual, physical need to see justice served.

I guess I had more of Mac in me than I realized.

"Come on." Shaw shoved inside a bagel joint. "We're eating breakfast."

"Now?" I tugged against him. "We've only got four hours left."

"You need to eat." He studied the menu board. "How about a bacon, egg and cheese bagel?"

I recognized that tone. It was easier to humor a man on a mission than to argue with one.

"Yes, that sounds delicious." I nudged him into line. "Make it a double, and let's go."

He dragged me closer and bent to my ear. "You need something to settle your stomach."

"My stomach is fine." I turned so our noses touched. "Have you lost your ever-loving mind?"

"When I feed," he said quietly, "the women are always starving after."

I thumped his ear. "Have you ever considered it was the sex and not the feeding?"

Embarrassment blossomed across his cheeks, even painting the tips of his ears bright red.

"Huh." I studied him. "I expected a bigger ego from an incubus."

Releasing me, he shifted his stance and waited. "Do you want the bagel or not?"

"Yes." I sighed. "We can figure out our next step while we eat."

"The boggart changes things." He placed our order, added a coffee and a tall frappé then paid. If travel expenses weren't on the conclave's dime, I might have argued. "We assumed Mrs. Richardson would fly straight home once she was cut loose in Odessa, but that might not be the case. She would trust the boggart to do exactly what it did—conceal incriminating evidence and refuse to speak with us until she was present. That frees her up to head straight for her office on the other side of town."

"Office?" I dropped into a sleek wooden chair at a table affording us a view of the Richardsons' building. "I thought she worked from home. I didn't see any copies of lease paperwork in her file."

"The building is in her husband's name. He owns it outright, but it's the address she uses on her invoices." The arrival of our food interrupted him. The waitress beamed at him, but Shaw only had eyes for me. The poor girl left in a huff. I smiled politely at her, but she didn't take that well either. "With the ranch in ashes and a boggart protecting her apartment, our last hope is they got sloppy at the office."

He passed me my food and set out my coffee before serving himself and sliding the tray onto the table next to ours. While unwrapping my bagel, I felt his gaze on me. "I'm fine." I lifted my hand. "I have some joint pain, the skin burns, but it's fading. I'll pop some ibuprofen and be as good as new."

"That can't happen again." He punished his sandwich with a sharp bite. "It's too dangerous."

"Which part?" I picked off a piece of bacon and nibbled on it. "The feeding or the kissing?"

After coughing into his fist, Shaw gulped his scalding coffee rather than answer.

"Here's the problem." I waited for his full attention. "I like you. At the risk of sounding twelve, I think you like me too. Whatever this is between us isn't going away just because you told it to. If it was that simple, we wouldn't be having this chat. You would have ditched those feelings a long time ago and lost the guilt I see in your eyes when you look at me." When he could breathe again, I forged ahead. "I get that I'm young by fae standards. I'm young by human standards too, but I'm not a little girl. I stopped being a kid the night I killed my friends. I'm not innocent. I'm not fragile. If you think for one minute I'm letting you kiss me and then walk away, you've been sniffing your own lure for too long."

Shaw sat there staring at me like he had never seen me before in his life. Maybe I shouldn't have mentioned the crush. Maybe I should have let him off the hook. Maybe I should have smiled through OJT and then freed him. Let him have his old life back. Let him hop in his truck and pursue his own dreams. Let the only contact we had be in the office or as we passed one another in the hall.

"Okay," he said.

The frappé I had reached for slid out of my hand. "Okay?"

"We're both adults. We can…" he swallowed hard, "…try."

"You date women all the time." I had watched the parade from my dorm window. "It'll be fine."

"I don't date." He scratched at a dry mustard spot on the table. "I don't—I just don't."

His palm was damp when I set my hand in his. "Trying sounds good."

Shaw looked pale as he tucked into his meal. Not hungry pale, plain old queasy.

I picked up my sandwich and ate while butterflies pirouetted in my stomach.

With both of us battling to keep our breakfasts down, I had to question what exactly we had agreed to.

CHAPTER TEN

With the world's most awkward breakfast behind us, Shaw and I returned to our rental car. I put myself in charge of plugging the office district address into my phone's GPS. When a man says he has a good idea of where he's going, I suggest having directions ready for when he inevitably realizes he doesn't.

Fifteen minutes of listening to a digitized voice chirp commands brought us to Sovereign Row.

The area was industrial, lots of tin and steel sheeting, but the Richardsons' warehouse was brick and mortar. A lush strip of lawn in an elevated planter splashed color against an ocean of concrete.

"Any word from Odessa?" I unbuckled and swung my bag across my shoulders.

His lips compressed as he checked his phone. "None yet."

Our eyes met, transmitting a shared sense of unease without saying a word.

We stepped out of the car and scanned the empty parking lot before approaching the side door.

While I kept watch against windblown burger wrappers, Shaw used his all-key to gain access.

"I have got to get me one of those," I mumbled.

"Guard the door." He crossed the threshold into the building. "I'll clear the space then circle back for you."

I peered into the gloom where rolled-up carpets lined the walls like Aladdin's version of a thrift-shop paradise.

"Not happening." I followed a step behind him. "Last time I let you he-man through a building without me, you ended up flat on your back with second-degree burns covering your entire left side."

"That chimera came out of nowhere," he deadpanned.

I arched one of my eyebrows in response.

With a deliberate motion, he reached behind me and shut the door on my heels, inserting himself into my personal space. He lingered there with his arm propped behind my back, leaning toward me.

Suddenly I had trouble breathing. Damn my sensitive nose. The dust in here was killer.

A slight grin touched his lips. "According to cached pages from around the time of purchase, this place was renovated before Mr. Richardson bought it two years ago. Four office suites, each with its own half bath, a full kitchen and four dock doors sum up the amenities. I doubt it's changed since."

I sidestepped out of his hold and locked down my hormones. I had a job to do.

"Good to know." I filled my lungs with musty air. "Smells clear to me. Nothing fae."

A slim dagger glinted in his hand. He must have palmed it from his bag. "Follow my lead."

Easing through the suite, I let my gaze wander. In addition to the rolled-up carpets were bolts of fabric, drapery material was my guess, and thick coffee-table-style books crammed with wallpaper samples extending past the binding. A brass plaque screwed into the outer door read Suite D. Three more to go.

Suite C opened into a collection of antique bedroom pieces with assorted tables thrown into the mix. Suite B was even less remarkable. Lamps sat on the floor against the walls. Sofas and loveseats occupied the center of the room. A few desks huddled in a corner. On the whole it reminded me of a staging warehouse full of stock for the fancy model homes Mom had loved to visit when I was a kid.

The kitchen sat opposite of Suite B, so we cleared it next. Empty cupboards, empty fridge. The sink carried the faint smell of rot and soy sauce. I checked the cabinets beneath it. Garbage disposal. For the scent to linger, somebody was using the place. Two weeks tops and that smell would be gone.

Shaw ducked out to check the last bathroom, leaving me to reach Suite A first. "The door's locked."

"Huh." He jiggled the knob upon his return. "The door is locked."

I cupped a hand to my ear. "Is there an echo in here?"

All-key in hand, he aimed for the lock. Metal screeched against metal. Second try, same result. "That has never happened before."

"It must be spelled." I pursed my lips. "Do you have the supplies to break a hex?"

"Several." He patted his messenger bag. "It all depends on who or what Richardson wanted kept out."

"She hasn't taken any anti-fae measures so far." I smoothed my left palm over the door. Tingles swept up my wrist when I gripped the knob, but the frame itself felt magic-free. "Stand back for a minute."

With him out of the way, I turned sideways and kicked the door about a foot beneath the knob.

"That's not going to work." Shaw rifled through his bag. "Nothing is that easy."

Starting to think he might be right, I gave it a second kick. Frustrated, I went for a quick third.

He pulled out a plastic bag of herbs and a lighter. "I hate to say I told you so, but—"

Fourth kick was the charm. Wood splintered, and the cheap door swung inward.

"Me too." I tossed a smile at him over my shoulder. "Luckily, my foot just said it for me."

"By the grace of the seven mothers," he murmured, tucking away his supplies.

My head whipped toward the room I had been too busy being smug to examine. Rookie mistake. The spelled door should have put me on guard against worse traps inside, but I had let Shaw distract me.

Rarity or not, I was starting to think the whole not-dating-coworkers rule was there for a reason.

Fumbling my cell out of my pocket, I tapped the flashlight app and cocked my head as the beam hit heavy plastic shrouding clunky shapes. Curiosity urged me into the room, guiding my hand. As I gripped the thick material, icy sensations rippled up my spine. Like to like, I sensed death here.

With a trembling hand, I ripped the sheeting from the nearest item then staggered backward with a scream lodged in my throat. Perfect glassy eyes stared at nothing. Silver hooves gleamed up at me.

"We were wrong." Shaw braced his hands on my shoulders when my back hit his chest.

"She wasn't belling." I swallowed the hard knot cutting off my oxygen. "This is…"

"I know." Rubbing circles on my back seemed to soothe him as much as it calmed me. "You don't have to go back in there."

Yes, I did. If I ran from this job, I was setting a precedent for cowardice the next time things got difficult.

"You handle inventory." The whisper of my voice gained force. "I'll catalog."

Might as well put the phone to use. Shock had fused it to my hand. My fingers refused to let go.

Warm lips brushed my temple. Shaw pressed the side of his face against mine, and I knew then I could survive this. A hard exhale stuttered from my lungs against his neck. I breathed in him instead.

Reluctant as I was, Shaw was the first to break away, to reenter the room, and I followed.

My phone's light beam helped me find a row of switches mounted to the wall by the door. I flipped several, and fluorescent light washed over us, illuminating the horrors of the room. I slumped against the wall, eyes drawn as if magnetized to the unicorn I had first uncovered. Its silver horn glinted. Dried blossoms twined with its sterling mane.

One by one, we uncovered them all.

Rare fae gazed numbly through painted eyes. They posed on wooden bases carpeted with grasses or peat, gruesome trophies on display. Brassy plaques identified each specimen, detailed the proud story of the beasts' origins and the scope of their abilities, as if the engraved reverence of those words mattered to them now.

Faint traces of magic shimmered in the air. Faded essence from the great powers these creatures had possessed in life all but abandoned them in death. They were tragic statues, each one frozen in its prime.

As the initial shock ebbed, a memory surfaced. "Shaw?"

He emerged holding a spiral notebook with a pen in his hand. "Are you okay?"

No, I wasn't. Judging by the dark shadows under his eyes, he wasn't either.

"This case is bigger than we thought." I dragged a hand down my face. "Should we be here? Should *I* be here? We aren't exactly inspectors. What if we're following the wrong leads?"

"We're part of a team," he assured me. "Mr. Richardson is being investigated by the team on the ground in Odessa. The ranch and this warehouse are the extent of his holdings. Between them and us, we have both Richardsons covered."

Nodding, I let him go back to his list-making while I began snapping pictures of the inventory.

I had to think of the victims as stock. I needed the mental distance.

Distance was good. Distance meant I could do my job without breaking down. Distance kept me too busy to connect the dots between what the Richardsons had done to these creatures and what my left palm and I did to the chimera. A living, fire-breathing, natural wonder, and I had skinned it alive.

A heavy weight landed on my shoulder, and I jumped as Shaw came to stand beside me.

"Don't." His thumb smoothed over my collarbone.

I pushed out the word. "What?"

"Make this about you." He led me forward into the shelter of his arms. "You're one of the good guys. You don't take innocent lives. You don't hurt innocent fae or people. You're a good marshal."

I buried my face against his hard chest, taking solace in his familiar scent. Not the earthy citrus one, the tempting lure, but his essence, bare skin that reminded me of sunrises and wet grass, new beginnings.

His chin dug into my scalp when he rested it on top of my head. "I don't know what's changing with your magic. The magistrates kept you suppressed for so long while you were in school, it's possible you have skills none of us suspect. We'll learn them as we go, okay?" He drew back to pin me with his gaze. "Even if this thing between us goes south, I'm always here for you, got that? Promise me that much, Thierry."

Numb as I was, his words couldn't hurt me. "You sound certain we're going to fail."

"Spectacularly," he said with a tender smile, "and I wouldn't miss it for the world."

His lips brushed over mine softly before he faded back into the dark corner of the room to work. I raised my phone's camera, grateful for the separation the screen gave me. Each tidy row of this grim exhibit exposed a new horror. A black mother púca and her litter huddled in their sleek rabbit forms. An emerald-haired mermaid sunned on a hollow rock, waiting on a tide that would never rise to carry her back out to the sea.

We lost hours in that room, poring over what Shaw had dubbed humanity's capacity for greed and cruelty. As fae, our hands were no less bloody. He and I were capable of committing worse acts.

Already my palm itched in anticipation of the judgments to come while the darker aspect of my nature pondered how human souls tasted. Would they be as filling as the chimera? Would the flavor be as rich? The effects last as long before my own hunger began gnawing my gut, begging to be fed?

Hesitating before a manticore, its human face twisted with rage on its lion's body, its enormous batlike wings unfurled in flight, its scorpion stinger poised over its spine, I snapped one last picture.

We were all monsters here.

CHAPTER ELEVEN

Down the street from the warehouse, Shaw and I found a coffee shop to hole up in until we got a confirmation from the marshals on the ground in Odessa that the Richardsons were heading our way.

We picked at bear claw pastries while staring at the phone on a napkin in the center of the table.

It mocked me with its blank display and distinct lack of flashing lights, so I thumped its screen.

"Feel better?" He spun his empty coffee cup on the edge of its base.

I huffed. "The phone had it coming."

"Clearly."

Flicking an almond off my Danish, I switched tactics. "How many marshals are on that team?"

"Marshal Johnathan Worth is handling the investigation into Mr. Richardson." His gaze touched on his phone. "He oversees evidence collection onsite. Maybe three others are bagging and tagging."

"Who's your contact?" I pressed.

"Worth," he answered. "I've worked with him before. Quiet guy. He's a dhampir."

"Half human and half vampire," I said slowly. "How does that work? Vamps are dead, right?"

"If you're thinking I asked him which of his parents was a necrophiliac, you're wrong."

Heat stung my cheeks. "Sorry, nothing should surprise me these days."

"You're young yet." He chuckled. "Wait until you've been a marshal for a few years."

Ignoring the age comment, I shelved my vampy curiosity for later. "Can you call anyone else?"

He shook his head. "I left a message for Mable when you went to the ladies' room."

"What?" Snow in July was almost as likely as Mable missing a phone call. "She didn't pick up?"

His cup spun a little faster. "It rang three times then rolled over to voicemail."

"I don't like this." I sank back in my chair. "What are we supposed to do?"

"Sit. Wait." He mirrored my position. "This is also part of the job."

"The boring parts were glossed over, much like Paperwork Mountain." I narrowed my eyes. "Is it too late to turn in one of those instructor-review forms? There were serious gaps in my education."

"This coming from the only person in her academy class who graduated," he said.

I shrugged. "If I hadn't wrecked the tower, more cadets might have reached the flag."

"No." His grin turned smug. "I had collected all the flags but yours."

A nervous pang tightened my chest. "Tell me that wasn't on purpose."

"You saw me," he said, voice rough. "It was all I could do not to..." He crushed the foam cup in his hand. "You earned your badge. Don't let anyone tell you any different. The magistrates sent Watchers in the event the results were contested. You were the only one who fought, did Mai tell you that? The other cadets handed me their kerchiefs." He snorted. "She threw hers in my face and ran."

I barked out laughter. "Mai did that?"

Massaging the base of his neck, he nodded. "Not everyone is as brave when faced with the hunger."

Not *his* hunger, but *the* hunger. I wasn't the only one who craved distance from myself.

"It's still you." I let him see I believed what I was saying. "Underneath it all, it's still you."

"You think so?" His gaze drifted toward the ceiling. "Sometimes I'm not so sure."

"Don't make me beat you with a hypocrisy stick." I leaned over the table and shoved him. "You don't get to give me fortune-cookie advice if I can't return the favor. Get your head out of your ass, bucko."

"Bucko?" A softening of his features told me he was amused. "Confidence is sexy on you."

"Yeah, well." I ducked my head to hide my tingling cheeks. "Fake it 'til you make it."

A sudden, urgent buzzing killed our conversation. Both of our gazes shot to his phone.

It was in his hand, at his mouth before I could intercept. "Shaw."

Eager for something to do, I scooped our trash onto a tray. I dumped it before grabbing my cup. May in Texas was hot. Not *bake your brain in your skull* temperatures like we saw in July and August, but I figured another round of drinks for the road wouldn't hurt. Though I might switch us to decaf.

Six cups of joe had Shaw's leg bouncing under the table. My finger tapping wasn't much better.

At the counter, I ordered two bottles of water. I hated the plain stuff, so back at the table I doctored mine up with a packet of the kiwi-strawberry flavored powder I carried with me. Shaw declined with a shake of his head.

"What do you mean?" He massaged his temples. "People don't just disappear."

"The Richardsons?" That would explain the lack of update.

He made a hush gesture with his hands, which tempted me to snag his phone and get straight to the answers. Instead, I turned up my bottle and chugged water to flush the caffeine out of my jittery system.

As it became apparent I wasn't getting details out of him until the call ended, I blocked out what I could of his conversation. Counting red sprinkles on the inflatable donut behind the register helped distract me.

"Something's wrong."

A second passed before I registered Shaw had spoken to me.

"Mable said no one at the office has heard from the marshals in Odessa in the last twelve hours. She's organizing a group to drive up there now." He tapped his phone on the table. "No one has seen the Richardsons since they were released from custody. The marshal who tailed them is missing."

I tensed to stand. "What's our next move?"

"Five agents don't fall off the grid." He ran a hand over his mouth. "Not without help."

"Do you think the Richardsons took them out?" I frowned. "Are they capable of that?"

His voice lowered to a cutting whisper. "How can you ask that after what we saw?"

"The marshals would have looked human," I said just as softly. "They would have been wearing glamour. It's one thing to murder fae you can convince yourself are animals, or abominations. It's another to pull the trigger while you're staring down fae who look human, on two legs, at eye level."

He ground his teeth. Good. Our almost-relationship wouldn't survive another *humans are food* diatribe. Humans were not food. Fine, not *just* food. They were, well, they were...*people.*

An exhale whistled through his teeth. "We have an hour until we get an update."

"If the Richardsons were coming to Dallas, they'd be here by now." I frowned. "That means they should have tripped a perimeter spell. So either they're not coming or they're crashing somewhere under the radar."

"They've got money," he reminded me. "We're assuming they didn't hop a plane overseas."

"Fae law has a longer reach than mortal law," I countered. "Their lock spell was weak, but it was proof they're more magically capable than we anticipated. Then there are the missing marshals to consider."

"The spell failed." His leg kept bouncing. "It should have sealed the door to the frame."

"What if it wasn't meant to keep us out," I wondered aloud, "but to alert them if we got in?"

"They had to know we would search the warehouse. They didn't make any effort to hide it."

"What if that was the point?" I chewed on my thumbnail. "What if they counted on us following the obvious breadcrumbs while they were biding their time, waiting to be released from custody? What if what they're hiding isn't in the city?" I dug out my phone and dialed Mable. "I need the last-known whereabouts of the subjects and confirmation whether they returned to the ranch after their release if you've got it."

Shaw stared at me, waiting until I hung up before making a rolling gesture with his hand.

"She's calling me back." Stomach tight, I pushed out of my chair. "I could use some air."

He waited until we got outside and the sidewalk emptied, then he closed the gap so our elbows brushed with each step. "Those fae had to come from somewhere. The Richardsons couldn't procure them solo."

The same thought had occurred to me. "They were fencing for a poacher."

"Had to be." He let me pull a step ahead. "How is this poacher getting rare fae out of Faerie into Texas? There's only one tether between realms in the state, and it's anchored on conclave grounds."

Good question. No poacher had balls big enough to parade his conquests across conclave property. They must be using a tether outside the state that anchored to a more remote location. It might even be off-map.

"The chimera was alive." My steps slowed as it truly hit me. "That means they're smuggling live fae."

Shaw stopped beside me, an odd look on his face. "Predators have to eat." He pressed redial and brought his phone to his ear. "Hey, I need you to dig up sales records for the cattle. Find out if the ranch was self-supporting."

The familiar sound of Mable's voice drifted to my ears as she signed off with a huff.

I followed his reasoning. "You're thinking the ranch was a front."

"Predators like chimeras and manticores require massive amounts of fresh meat to keep them alive for any period of time. It makes sense that if the Richardsons were bringing in fae from out of state, they would do it in bulk. It takes time to process a body. More time if the fae are kept alive for other reasons."

Black-market vendors would sell their own mothers for fresh organs, horns, hooves, bones from rare stock. Sold to the right magic practitioner or initiated fanatic, those parts were worth their weight in gold. Even as small as Wink was, its back-alley streets housed a licensed Unseelie bazaar on the fae side of town.

"The question is where." We reached the parking deck adjacent to the apartment tower. "The ranch was destroyed."

"The house and the barn were destroyed," he corrected me as we searched the reserved guest spots for our car.

"Same difference." Or was it? "Do you remember the receipt for the construction of those storm shelters? Each of the five shelters on the property would have cost him around one hundred grand to build." A half million dollars buried underground. "It's excessive even by Tornado Alley standards."

"Underground holding cells?" Shaw jabbed the key fob, and our car chirped.

"We need to find out if the storm shelters were discovered and, if they were, whether they were searched. With a bill that high there must be blueprints floating around somewhere. At this point, I'd settle for a map showing their general vicinity on the property." I borrowed his pen. "I'll ask Mable when she calls."

"You do that." He started up and backed onto the street.

I looked up from my note-making. "What's with that tone?"

"I'm dropping you off at the hotel." He stomped on the gas. "You follow this lead."

The pen rolled out of my hand. "Where do you think you're going?"

"I'm going to disable the perimeter spells." At my puzzled glance, he added, "I have something better, but it takes time to arm them. The new hexes will track the Richardsons if they cross a warded threshold."

"Impressive. An incubus with a knack for spellwork." Most used their lures to get what they wanted. "I had no idea you were so handy."

"I slept my way through a coven once," he said in a detached voice. "I kept my eyes open and walked away three grimoires richer than when I got there."

If he was waiting for condemnation from me, we would be here for a while. I wasn't much for throwing stones, and all the panes had already been shattered in my glass house.

"Stop bragging." I rescued my pen from between the seats and began doodling in my notebook until his white-knuckled grip on the wheel eased. "I have work to do."

"I'll try to make it fast." He sounded hesitant, as if he didn't trust he had gotten off the hook so easily. "The sooner we leave the better."

"Leave?" I twisted to face him. "We're driving back to Wink?"

"No." His lips hitched into a half grin. "We're flying into Midland then driving to Odessa."

An hour. We could be on the ground in an hour. Two tops. "What if the conclave finds out?"

"Oh, they will." He winked. "I plan on them reimbursing our tickets."

"Shaw." My teeth worried that same thumbnail. "I'm still on probation for the next six months."

"I can't make the decision for you. It's your job if they don't buy into the asking-for-forgiveness-instead-of-permission bit."

I thought about that room, those fae and the humans who had profited from their misery.

"I have a confession to make. I've never flown before." The potential for fiery death had my stomach executing a double barrel roll. "We should probably grab Dramamine on the way to the airport."

Yeah. Because motion sickness was the worst of my problems.

CHAPTER TWELVE

After staggering off the plane, I made a beeline for the ladies' room while Shaw strode to the rental car desk to snag us a new set of wheels. We finished at the same time and met at the exit door.

"Here." He passed me an ice-cold bottle with a peach on the label. "This was all they had."

With a hand held in front of my mouth, blocking my breath, I accepted. "Much appreciated."

The first sip was god-awful. I hated peaches. I know, I know, take away my Southern belle card. At least swishing the water around my mouth got rid of the bile taste clogging the back of my throat.

While I was doing the good old rinse-and-spit routine, Shaw jingled a set of keys in his hand.

What can I say? He was a subtle kind of guy.

"Feel better?" A pack of gum rested on his open palm.

"Yeah." I took two hits of wintergreen and started feeling human again. Half human anyway.

He tossed the chunky keys then plucked them from the air. "Then let's get a move on."

Vibrations in my jeans pocket almost set off another round of dry heaving. "Hmph?"

"Thierry?" Mable's gentle voice was a balm to my raw nerves. "Are you all right?"

"Fine." I took another swig of vile peach water. "Just an upset stomach."

"Oh." She perked. "In that case, take some of the pink stuff, dear. It should do the trick."

I dredged up half a smile. "I'll do that."

Papers rustled in the background on her end. "Give me a minute. There. All right. I have the information you requested." Her exhale blasted the receiver. "I hope I'm not too late to be useful."

"You're fine. It's not like we could use our—" *phones on the airplane*, "—never mind."

She clicked her tongue. "Knowing Shaw, it's probably best I don't ask."

"I— Yeah." I didn't want to start lying to her. Shaw was a big boy. *He* could fess up when the time came.

"As for the information you requested..." she hummed while the familiar click-clacking noise of fingers on a keyboard filled the line, "...the Richardsons were last seen en route to their ranch by a marshal heading into town for lunch. He passed their car, recognized the subjects and called in the sighting. That's all I have there."

Considering our lack of contact point, I had to ask, "What happened to him?"

"That call is the last recorded contact we have on file for him."

A pang echoed through my chest. "What about the others?"

More clicking as her keyboard sang. "It looks like his call was the last documented contact from the ranch."

I blinked. "Before the second team arrived, you mean."

"No." She hesitated. "The second team hasn't responded in the last forty-five minutes."

"It's an hour drive to Odessa from Wink." I checked my phone. "It's been two hours."

"I know." Her voice lowered until I strained to hear her. "The magistrates have been informed."

Air hissed from between my teeth. Not good. Not good at all.

Mable recovered faster than I did. "Is Shaw with you?"

"Yes." I raised my voice so he would hear. "Shaw's here."

He turned at the sound of his name, brow furrowed as his gaze zeroed in on my phone.

"Save me a call and tell him the Richardsons' ranch hasn't turned a profit in the last five years. I can't find any records of sales made since then. However, the ranch has continued to participate as a buyer in several quarterly auctions." She hummed. "The ranch is three thousand acres with…it looks like…five hundred head at the ranch's peak ten years ago. Based on the records we confiscated from the Richardsons' accountant, almost six hundred feeder cattle were purchased in the last five years."

"Too bad there's no way to know how many cattle were there at the time of the fire." I added, "Without counting skulls I mean."

"Oh, but there is." Mable tittered. "A recent vet bill shows vaccinations for three hundred head."

"Well damn. Richardson wrote off eight hundred cattle, not counting what his own stock produced."

"Do I assume from your tone that's good news?"

"I'm not sure yet." I snapped my fingers. "Any luck finding blueprints for the storm shelters?"

"No." Her enthusiasm waned. "There are records of the costs and a breakdown of materials, but if blueprints existed, I figure they were either kept in the office at the ranch, or they were destroyed."

"You're probably right." Though I could guess, I still asked, "What was on the material list?"

"Steel," she said, "and lots of it."

Another sip of water made me wince. "I figured." Iron was the main ingredient in steel.

"Oh. An email from you just popped up in my inbox. Should I open it?"

"Well that took forever. It's picture heavy. I sent it before leaving Dallas. I guess it took a while for the…um…" *Crap.* I sucked at lying. I had to work on my poker face—poker voice? "The important thing is you got the message."

"You left Dallas?" Concern shot her voice up an octave. "Without telling me? Marshals are going missing. You don't change locations without calling here first."

"I, well…"

"Put Shaw on the phone," she snapped. "*Now.*"

With a scowl aimed at me with laser precision, he accepted the phone when I offered it to him.

I'll give him this much. He accepted his dressing-down like a man. A man whose eye twitch said he was counting backward from one hundred and that Mable wasn't the one making him grind his teeth.

Me and my big mouth.

Clamping a strong hand on my shoulder, he kept me from beating a hasty retreat and calling my cell a loss. Squirming got me exactly nowhere. Slight paling of his eyes shocked me into stillness. It was one thing for me to blab our location to Mable. It was another for Shaw to incubus-out in public.

"Yes, ma'am." Shaw grated out the words. "I'll take good care of her."

I tried looking contrite. "Well?"

He tossed my phone at me. "Mable threatened to lose my paychecks for life if I let you get hurt. Again."

"Aww." I pocketed the cell. "That's sweet."

He fisted the front of my shirt and dragged me up against him. "That mouth of yours."

I wet my lips. "Yes?"

His eyes crushed shut as their color faded to white. "It's going to get you in trouble one day."

"Probably," I agreed. "But that day is not today."

His growl barely registered within my hearing.

"Here." I stepped beside him and looped my arm around his waist. "Let's get you to the car."

Tucking me closer against his side, he leaned into me. "I didn't hurt you, did I?"

"No." Bruises healed too fast to fret over them.

His grunt sounded unconvinced. "You sent Mable everything?"

"All our notes, pictures and pertinent file information. She just confirmed receipt."

"Good." After a few test blinks, he opened copper eyes. "Still no word from the ground?"

"None." I stared up at him. "This whole thing stinks to high heaven."

"Yeah, it does. Someone has to go to that ranch and find out what the hell is going on out there." He twisted until he faced me. "This situation goes beyond anything you were trained to face. I can't ask you to square off against these people." His surly expression gentled. "I want you to consider sitting this one out."

I laughed. Hard. Until my eyes watered.

He didn't so much as crack a smile.

"You aren't serious." I waited for him to tell me I was hearing him wrong. "We're partners."

"Whatever the Richardsons have out at that ranch is taking down seasoned marshals."

"You don't think I'm good enough." Coming from him…that hurt.

"We've lost a quarter of the marshals out of our office." He dragged a hand through his hair. "According to Mable, I'm the highest-ranking marshal in the vicinity. That makes me interim divisional commander, and I'm not blindly ordering more of our people to their deaths." His jaw flexed. "The Southeastern Conclave is on standby, and I've asked Mable to prep another team. But they won't be dispatched until I've gotten a look around. I need to give the others an idea of what we're up against so they can prepare." He hesitated, trying to temper his next words. "That's why I can't ask you to go. It's a solo mission."

I read between the lines. "A suicide mission you mean."

"Thierry." He kept using that placating tone. "I don't plan on going anywhere."

"Good." I wiped my sweaty palms on my jeans, then pasted on the syrupy-sweet smile I usually reserved for con jobs on Mom. "Then you won't mind me not going anywhere with you."

"Stubborn." Eyes flickering to white, he lowered his head, parted his lips.

"You're going to try to kiss me with that mouth? After what you just said?" I jabbed the unlock icon on the key fob dangling from his fingers then shoved him back. "Dream on, Shaw."

While he grumbled, I got in the car. By the time I got the nervous flickers in my palm under control, Shaw slid behind the wheel with a grunt. I strapped in and pulled up the GPS.

Ready or not, here we come.

CHAPTER THIRTEEN

Chewed-up bits of asphalt crunched under our tires as Shaw guided the rental car off the uneven shoulder of the road. A slim green mile marker staked out the ground ten feet from the front bumper.

"Proceed for one point two miles," a computerized voice urged.

I killed the navigation prompt and leaned back against the headrest.

Silence filled the car to bursting.

"There's still time to change your mind." Shaw's fingers tightened around the steering wheel.

I told him the truth. "I've changed it at least six times since we left the airport."

His white-knuckled grip relaxed a fraction. "And?"

"I can't let you go alone."

A slow nod left his head hanging as though he expected a guillotine blade to fall.

Reaching behind my seat, I retrieved our satchels from the floorboard. I dropped his onto his lap, turning away while I did a cursory check through mine to hide my trembling fingers from his sight.

Once I forced my tremors under control, I shoved open the door and stepped out of the car. "Let's do this."

His response was to join me on the sandy strip near the highway, underneath the glaring sun. Laughter tickled the back of my throat when he locked the rental behind us, like he was making the statement we would be back and that he didn't want to be liable if someone stole it. Optimism. I liked that.

"I'm texting Mable our location now." Calling her would have been too hard. I might have said something stupid, like goodbye. Texting kept me calm, kept those fears expanding my chest bottled.

Another nod, this one as distracted as the first. He slung his bag across his body and started walking.

"Here we go," I murmured.

There was no traffic, no sound except for our footsteps, the shift of sand and the occasional grind of asphalt or concrete or litter underfoot. A tickle of unease had me stifling nervous giggles. I was not a giggler. But the lack of cars, lights, sirens— anything—sent creepy sensations crawling down my nape.

"That must have been the first checkpoint." He jerked his chin toward an unmarked car covered with an odd sheen. It looked like someone had taken a handful of Crisco shortening and smeared it over the hood. The tires on the right side looked flat. No. They were still inflated, but buried in sand. The whole car tilted to that side. Doors stood open. Soft country music drifted to my ears. The engine was running.

I took a step toward the car. "Should we…?"

Shaw's hand clamped over my upper arm. "Leave it."

Dusty air filled my lungs as I scented the area. "No blood. That goo—it's definitely fae."

"No marshal goes down without a fight." He grimaced. "Whatever got to him, it got there fast."

After surveying the area, I noted the nearest structure, the only one untouched by the fire, was a pump house.

"Stay put." Shaw flicked his wrist, unleashing his claws as he released me. "Watch my back."

For once I didn't argue. Muscles tense and palms damp, I waited as he searched the small building.

"Clear," he called. "Let's go."

Nodding, I drifted toward him, shoring up my nerves. I liked to run my mouth and play at being a badass, but the bottom line was both our asses were on the line out here. I was young. I was inexperienced. I didn't know it all, and if I thought too hard about it, my fear would take control.

Pangs radiated through my chest, like my vital organs wanted to bust out of their cage and hotfoot it back to the car. A hand over my thundering heart made me wince. I rubbed the spot like it would make a difference.

This was real. We were here. Evidence suggested the other marshals were dead or taken. That left Shaw and me to stop whatever horror the Richardsons had harnessed and taught to pop marshals into its mouth like M&M's. By the time we reached the driveway, spots danced on the edges of my vision and breathing was like trying to gulp air with my lungs full of water. I was ready to tuck tail and run, and the fear pissed me off.

I had done bad things. I would do worse one day I was sure. But I had done good too, and this was my fight. I had trained for this. It was my job to make the Richardsons pay for the lives they had taken. Fae or human didn't matter. Seeing justice done—that was important. Come hell or high water, I was doing this.

"Here we are." Shaw stopped where the road dipped and turned from blacktop to dust.

Straight as an arrow, the dirt road shot toward where the Richardsons' house once stood. Acres of green pasture rolled as far as the eye could see in either direction. Ahead, the charred bones of the once-lavish house glared at those who dared to visit, to see it reduced to such bitter leavings. Beyond that, the blackened skeleton of the main barn stood watch over smoldering stalls on a burnt patch of grass.

With a growl, Shaw stalked toward the nearest gatepost. "This should have been the second checkpoint."

Spent shell casings littered the ground. A rifle stuck to the post he examined, covered by opaque slime. He swiped a finger through the thickest bit, hissing a string of swears as he wiped off the goo.

"What's wrong?" Unidentified fae ooze could mean any number of things.

"It stings." He rubbed his finger through the dirt. "Reminds me of a mild acid burn."

"Any idea what it could be?"

He straightened and dusted his hands. "No clue."

"Those checkpoints..." I jerked my chin toward the last one. "Were they maintained by the backup units?"

"They had to be." He exhaled. "The first responders hadn't reported anything unusual. Most weren't armed."

Unarmed meant different things to different fae, but most shunned guns and modern weaponry.

"This should be fun." Flat as the area was, the Richardsons could literally see us coming from a mile away. Based on the evidence at hand, they had one nasty welcome wagon ready to roll over us.

When I stepped from the road onto the driveway, the thick soles of my sneakers sank in the sand and turned my foot. *Stupid ankle.* Thrown off balance, I flung out my arms and braced for the fall, landing on all fours. That was when I felt it, a slight trembling under my left palm.

"Do you feel that?" I reared up, scanning the area, hearing nothing, seeing nothing.

In my periphery, Shaw shrugged. "I don't know what you're talking about."

"I don't hear it now." Stinging in my palm made me wince. Blood smeared my hand where I must have landed on a rock. Before the cut closed, instinct guided me to place the wound to the earth. Sound exploded in my head. "Something's coming. Something big."

A shudder wracked Shaw, the start of his change. "I don't see anything."

Filling my lungs only made me cough. "I don't smell anything, either."

"I got nothing." He knelt beside me, bracing his palm flat on the ground. "Are you sure?"

"I don't know." I dusted my hands. "My magic has been on the fritz lately. I'm not sure if it's—"

The rumbling became audible. Tremors made the ground quake beneath our knees. Dirt erupted, and a dusky appendage burst upward, spraying sand. The conical tip swung left to right, hesitating as runes flared in my palm. The stout column swayed, lowering, following that burst of frantic light.

"What the hell is that?" I squeaked.

"It's an annuli." Shaw's hand clamped down on my arm. "Don't make any sudden moves."

Muscles quivered in my thighs, twitching with the urge to run. "Is that Latin for 'giant worm'?"

"Close enough." His stance tensed. "It shouldn't be able to track us this well aboveground."

Its segmented skin faded from a swarthy rose color to near translucence around the area protruding from the ground. "It doesn't have eyes." I flattened my palm to help my balance, and the thing's head rotated to one side. *Crap.* A vague memory of a gross earthworm dissection in my sophomore year surfaced. "It's the light."

"Receptors in its skin cells," Shaw agreed. "It can detect light and changes in light intensity."

"So it can't see us," I reasoned, "but it can track our movement using our shadows if we run."

Except—lucky me—I had a beacon in my palm, making me easy to spot.

"Something like that." He studied its swaying bulk. "It can't hear, but it can sense vibrations."

Thinking of how quickly it had pinpointed us, I swallowed hard. "Magic or otherwise?"

"I'm guessing," he said, lowering his voice despite himself, "but I'll go with both."

I groaned. "What you're saying is we're screwed."

"Pretty much."

The annuli continued swaying like a cobra ready to strike, with what, I wasn't sure. No eyes, no ears— was it too much to hope the giant worm didn't have a mouth filled with sharp teeth either?

Ripples worked through its neck, like a cough with nowhere to go.

And then the tip of its head split in two.

"You've got to be joking." I tried to look away, but stared transfixed as its gaping mouth parted. The annuli's hacking cough worsened, deepened. Like idiots, Shaw and I knelt there watching it all. After a few more tries, it hocked up a glob of white mesh hanging from a thick cord down its, well, it didn't have a chin. The odd bundle dripped familiar opaque goo. "It looks like a melting spider web made out of gooey string."

"New plan." Shaw didn't wait for it to slurp the mesh back into its mouth. "Run."

He jumped to his feet and jerked me so hard after him my knees left the ground. Stumbling, I gained my balance in time for the annuli to vomit—its tongue?—at us. Spittle from the tongue flecked the backs of my arms with liquid agony as it smacked into the ground on my heels.

"Does this new plan have a next step?" I panted. "We can't outrun it forever."

"I'm working on it," he growled.

The driveway stretched for maybe half a mile ahead of us. The rental car sat about that far in the opposite direction. The abandoned car was closer, unlocked, which made it a damn tempting refuge. But I wasn't sure how much the annuli would swallow to get to us, and all I needed was to be caught Googling *How to Hot-wire A Car in Sixty Seconds or Less* when it showed up, flung its drool-covered net over the car and gulped down the whole thing. Any way you cut it, death by digestion sounded disgusting.

Hard-packed dirt split beneath our feet. Sand bubbled through the cracks when the annuli passed under us. Its tunnel bowed the road, making our feet sink into the shifting debris trail. Heavier than I was,

Shaw sank to the ankle in the freshly tilled soil. I clamped my fingers around his belt, steadying him until he caught his balance. While I kept hold of him, I led him toward the fence and the pasture.

"We need more room," I yelled by way of explanation.

"It won't help." Planting a palm on the nearest fence post, he vaulted over it. "Thierry?"

Barbed wire raked the inseam of my jeans when I leapt. Unlike Shaw, my landing didn't stick. My ankle was still tender and it turned, sending me sprawling into the grass on all fours. The same raw power as before seeped into my palm, flipping a switch in my pain-addled brain and launching my darker self into the foreground of my mind with a snarl. Pressure built in my head. Familiar hunger set my stomach cramping.

I had experienced this out-of-body sensation before, a tangible awareness splitting plain old Thierry from the Black Dog's heir. As it had with the chimera, some internal set of scales began shifting, searching for balance, weighing my life and Shaw's against the annuli's. Seconds later, the uneasiness vanished, and only a cold resolve remained.

My hunger wasn't like Shaw's. It wasn't set by a clock. It didn't follow a pattern. It didn't crave a thing I could supply to slake its yearning. My need wasn't a whisper in my subconscious, haunting me all the time like his. It burned hotter, struck faster, goaded me nearer to the edge until I tumbled.

The fall was white-hot bliss burning through my palm.

Shaw grabbed me by the elbows, lifting me onto my feet and dragging me after him.

"We can't keep going like this," I wheezed, breathless from the magic swirling inside me.

"What's the alternative?" he snapped. "Stop and let it eat us? No thanks."

"No. Not you." I swung my leg out and tripped him. "Me."

Momentum carried him crashing to the ground. Turning my back on him, I faced the worm and spread my arms. The wait was a short one. Vibrations underground jarred my teeth. A plume of dust spat at the sky as the annuli rose into the air and towered above me. "Come and get it," I screamed, waving my glowing palm.

The worm belched its net over me. *That is so nasty.* Sticky and slimy like those hand-shaped toys you got for a quarter out of vending machines at the grocery store. Where its saliva touched me, I burned. I had a nice crosshatch pattern going before he started slowly reeling me toward his mouth.

"Are you insane?" Shaw sank his fingers into the tongue and latched on. "Get out of there."

"Let me go." Or both of us would die. "I got this."

Understanding widened his eyes. "This thing is huge. You can't take it down by yourself."

"We don't have a choice." I sank my elbow into his gut. "Trust me."

With a furious snarl that raised hairs down my nape, he released the net. His jaw set and his fists clenched, but he let me go. I turned my back on him before I lost my nerve and found myself facing the worm's gullet.

As it dragged me past its liplike folds, it began coughing again. This time it spat stomach acid that splashed me, burning so much worse than the mesh ever had. Skin blistered and welts rose. The smell made my eyes water. As its mouth closed around me, the annuli jerked its tongue, and I fell onto its bottom jaw. Feeding every ounce of power I had into my palm, I flattened that glowing hand flush with its skin.

Hissing and writhing, the annuli slung its head, slamming me against the walls of its throat. The length of my body caught sideways in its craw, and it choked. Ripples in its skin pulsated beneath my hand. Sunlight flashed in my eyes as its maw gaped open. With a wet hack, the annuli horked me onto the ground. Two bodies came hurling out after me in a mound of mucus, both partially digested.

I recoiled, scuttling backward until I locked down my panic. The bodies of the fallen marshals gave me strength to stand. While the annuli flailed and spat, I ran straight for it, leapt onto its throat and pressed my runes back into its slimy skin. Its scream rang in my ears as ravenous magic jolted its heart, no *hearts*. Five massive organs all lined up in a neat row down its center. Power blazed through each, shocking them out of sync like the annuli had gulped a live wire.

Its soul was scattered, pockets of it lingering behind each pulsing beat, and my magic writhed in those nooks and crannies, chomping down on that sweet, dark energy until my body hummed with it, until my senses were bloated with a crazed hyperawareness.

Fueled by the meal, I sent scissoring blasts of power sliding under its skin. It cried out once more, a horrid sound that faded as its soul extinguished and my internal scale balanced. Too late to call back what I had unleashed, I clung to the body of the annuli until its skin peeled and fell over me, drying to a ringed husk that crinkled as I batted it away. The creature's flesh quivered for a minute, its tiny brain realizing too late that it was dead, before the column thumped onto the ground.

Tangled in yards of peeling skin, I leapt aside. Not far enough. The stout neck rolled, crushing my right foot before I could crawl out of its path. I was lying there, screaming, when Shaw bent over me and shoved a ball of fabric into my mouth to muffle my shouts. I bit down, gnashing my teeth and clawing the annuli.

Throwing his shoulder against the worm, Shaw slammed into its corpse until I could scoot from under it. Backed a safe distance from its still-twitching body, I fell onto the ground in a sobbing heap. Tears veiled my eyes, but I saw Shaw, pale skin clashing against the green grass and blue sky.

"Focus."

I shook my head. I couldn't hear. It hurt too much.

His hands cradled my face, and he removed the gag. "Lock down the pain so you can heal."

The next shake of my head was feebler.

"You're shaking." He forced my gaze to his. "You took too much. Your body can't process so much energy."

That explained the sensation of being stuffed with sizzling light that wanted to blast out of my pores.

"Hurts," I managed.

"I know." His thumbs swept across my cheekbones. "Come on, Thierry, focus for me."

My eyes watered. Shaw's touch centered me, anchored me while I pushed the strange new magic swirling in my system toward my injuries. Power fused the broken bones. Muscles snapped back into place. The burst of agony as my body mended sent shock waves rippling up my leg and shivering through my torso. It jarred my heart and zoomed up my neck to my head. Faint sparks danced on the ends of my hair.

"I need to…" I pushed upright, slurring drunkenly as I rotated my ankle. "Hey, I thought that was broken."

The smile touching Shaw's lips didn't reach his eyes. "I have to take you down a few notches."

I laughed, giddy from the high of surviving, the rush of feeding, the sweet ache of being so close to him. Throwing my arms around his neck, I tugged him over me as I flopped down to the plush bed of grass.

He surrendered with a pained groan, as though the flurry of jade sparkles in my hair had ignited the beast in him, reaching deep inside, past his defenses, drawing his monster out to play with mine.

Skin already pale faded. Razor claws elongated, thickening, curving to spear into the ground beside my head where he braced himself over me. Even his canines elongated at the corners of his mouth in a savage way that sent anticipation trembling through my lower stomach. My hand rested on his shoulder. It was so easy sliding it down his chest, over the buckle of his belt.

"Don't," he begged me. "Not like this."

"I don't think I can stop," I confessed on a ditzy laugh. "I need you." His touch was my anchor, his skin and his scent the only things able to stop me from shattering into a million sun-drenched pieces.

"I know." He pressed a lingering kiss to my forehead. "But not in that way."

Before I could argue, he captured my wrist, joined his right hand with my left one and threaded our fingers together. I jerked against his iron grip as the grim set of his mouth penetrated the cottony haze stuffing my head.

"This is going to hurt," he said.

I caught lightning in my palm. That's how it felt as he bled the excess magic from me into himself. My gut burned and my heart stuttered as I weakened. His need was nothing gentle, nothing caring. It was endless and miserable, mindless and reckless. At that moment I was all that existed in his bleak world, all he craved, the best thing he had ever tasted and the one meal he wanted to savor forever.

His stream of consciousness seared my brain for days, or maybe it was seconds, before my mind shorted out and the world spluttered from full color to a static flicker. Soon even that twinkle faded to an icy-cold black.

CHAPTER FOURTEEN

Waking in a small room in a wet puddle left me more confused than the half-baked dreams I left behind. Faint light spilled from my hand, illuminating a water pump and a pressure tank near my leg. Humming from a motor droned in my ears, a not-so-nice counterpoint to the ringing already there.

Muck squished under my hand when I pushed upright. "What's that smell?"

"Manure," a rough voice answered from the darkness opposite me.

I angled toward the sound, blinking while my eyes adjusted. "Where are we?"

"The pump house," Shaw answered.

Mentally I tallied our position. "Halfway between the start of the driveway and the rental car."

"Mmm-hmm." Metal jingled. Keys dangled from the ring looped around his middle finger. Shaw stared through a crack in the door, gaze sweeping from side to side.

Rotating my ankle, I winced. "That's not a subtle way of asking me to wait in the car, is it?"

His hand closed and the rattling ceased. "I didn't say anything."

"That makes it easier to forgive and forget what you implied." I settled some weight on my foot. "Forgiving is tough. Forgetting is easier." I hissed as I stood. "That might be brain damage talking."

He cracked a smile. "I can't tell any difference."

I made a face at him. "What are the odds the Richardsons have another annuli on patrol?"

"Zero," he answered a beat later. "They're too territorial to even share land with a mate."

"Good." I shuddered. "If I never see another one, it will be too soon." Shaw turned from his post to study me limping around the tiny room's edge. "How do you think the Richardsons controlled it?"

"Annuli minds are small and easily influenced. A simple spell would do the trick."

The more I walked, the looser my ankle became and the less it twinged. "How long was I out?"

"Twenty minutes." His expression softened. "How do you feel?"

"Like the worm after the early bird got through with it." I frowned. "No, that's not right."

His warm chuckle calmed my nerves. He pulled my phone from his jeans. "Mable emailed."

"Good news?" I took the cell, thumbed the email icon and grinned. "Very good news."

"Anything you want to share with the rest of the class?"

"Cute." I snorted. "She sent a scan of a map of the Richardsons' property."

"And?"

Two blue dots sat inches apart. "There are two locations marked for storm shelter installation."

"I thought there were no records?" He folded his arms. "How reliable is her information?"

"Apparently the Richardsons went all out. They added plumbing in two of them." I forwarded a copy of the email to him. "They needed permission from the local water company to run the pipes. It looks like the water company has an easement on the property, so they kept a record for future use."

His fingers spread over his phone's screen, enlarging the image. "Which looks more promising to you?"

"The one on the right is close enough to the main house to have been a storm shelter. Every inch of the foundation was pored over by the investigating team before they started vanishing. Anything unusual would have been found and reported." After taking the second dot and our relative position into account, I tapped the screen. "The other is positioned several acres from the house and offers more privacy."

"With the annuli guarding the property line," he mused, "they could afford to retreat deeper into their acreage."

"Okay." I slid my phone into my back pocket. "Let's go."

"I'm only going to ask this once." Blocking the door, Shaw faced me. "Are you sure you're—?"

"Don't make me hurt you." I walked up and jabbed the center of his chest. "It'll look bad on my performance evaluation." Grazing him on my way through the door, I scowled. "Don't count me out yet."

His breath blasted my nape. "You're like a dog with a—"

My elbow shot back and sank in his gut. I'm lucky I didn't break something on those abs of his. While he coughed manfully over my shoulder, I studied the flat, grassy terrain between us and our objective.

Resisting the urge to rub my elbow, I stepped outside the relative safety of the pump house. "Are we just going to walk up to them?"

"We don't have much choice." He sounded pained. "Last time I checked, neither of us had mastered any covert glamour skills. We can't mask stationary objects from view, let alone obscure moving ones."

The man had a point. "If they see us coming, that gives them more time to prepare."

"They've already fallen back. They're in their safe place." His teeth flashed. "They're trapped."

The predator in me roused, still hyped from the kill. "They're in a defensive position."

"No, they're in a box in the ground." That toothy smile grew a tad sharper. "And they've got to get air from somewhere."

"What does—?" Tempting spice hit my nose, the scent of his skin intoxicating. It backed me up a step, until my shoulders hit his chest. Understanding pierced the fog rousing my libido. "Oh, I like the way you think."

CHAPTER FIFTEEN

No two ways about it. The Richardsons knew we were coming. Even if they hadn't figured out I had decommissioned their guard worm, it stood to reason that if the annuli had first become aware of our presence because we had tripped a perimeter spell, then the Richardsons also knew of the breach.

Yet for all that, the walk was uneventful. The most excitement we had was dodging cow patties.

A warm breeze ruffled my hair, drying the sweat running down my nape. The hike into cow country did my foot good. It stopped aching, but the skin felt too tight, like the time Andrea dumped a bottle of Elmer's over my toes then sprinkled an entire box of emerald glitter over the top.

Hey, when you're five and don't have access to nail polish, bad things can happen.

That flicker of memory, even though it was a happy one, pierced my heart. Andrea, my first best friend, dead because of me, because she was the first to touch the light kindling in my hand.

"Is your foot hurting?" Shaw rested his hand between my shoulder blades.

"No." I rubbed the tender center of my chest. "It's fine. I'm fine."

The look he shot me called me ten kinds of liar, but he didn't press me.

"The dot didn't look so far away on the map," I grumbled.

"We're almost there." His steps were light, his expression clear. Almost serene. Tense as he had been the whole trip, for days really, I doubted the annuli's demise was the reason for his newfound calm. "Keep up."

As he set off ahead of me, I hung back admiring the view. The man knew how to wear jeans, and his shirt was missing a six-inch strip around the bottom where he had ripped it before using it to gag me. The dirty thoughts his rear view and peekaboo abs inspired caused a light bulb to flash over my head.

No wonder Shaw was Mr. Zen. He had fed. A lot. On *me*.

He was at peace, if only for a little while, and I had given that to him. He had helped me out too. Without him, I would still be flying as high as a kite and batting at the clouds like a kitten on catnip.

"Take a look at this." Shaw stood with his hands resting on his hips, staring at something on the ground the high grass hid from me. He kicked out his boot, and metal clanged. "I think we found it."

"I think you're right," I agreed as a three-by-six-foot steel door inset into a concrete pad came into view. The surface was smooth. Its hinges must be to the inside. The handle, and there must be one, was hidden. Two feet of concrete framed the door. Sod covered the rest of the concrete lid, giving us no clue how much hollow mass spread beneath us. All we had was an access point we couldn't, well, access.

"Stand back and keep watch," Shaw ordered. "I'm going to find the intake vent."

Twenty yards away he whistled and knelt. Rising onto my tiptoes, I shielded my eyes against the glare from a whirling silver turbine.

From here, Shaw looked like any guy resting on his knees in the grass, but the tingle in my nose told me the truth. Standing slightly downwind from his position meant his lure drifted past on the edge of my periphery. His scent made sweat bead on my forehead and roll into my eyes.

Never had it occurred to me to wonder where his scent glands were, how his lure was produced. If he kept this up much longer, I would be forced to explore answers to those questions with my tongue.

Snap out of it.

I held my breath until I regained coordination of my limbs then eased out of the path of his enticing scent.

With a tight nod at me, he stood and dusted off his jeans. His first order of business was punting the spinning turbine downfield. Sound wasn't a concern as he crushed the base with his heel. Taking off the shredded remains of his shirt, he balled the fabric and shoved it down the tube before kicking dirt into the hole. The air shaft was clogged. Even if they had a second intake, the circulation was hampered, sealing the Richardsons in with the tempting fragrance of an incubus male in his prime.

Or so we hoped.

Ten minutes passed. Twenty. Shaw gave them thirty minutes before crossing back to me.

"It didn't work." He surveyed the area while I worked hard at not surveying his shirtless state. "They must have a filtration system."

Forcing my girly bits to behave, I tamped down the lure's effect. This was not the time nor the place to get frisky. "Let's give it another minute."

Just like a man, he took me literally. "Time's up. We should fall back and work a new angle."

We cleared a dozen yards before a pinging sound made me whip my head around. I shoved Shaw behind me, which made him snarl and forced me to elbow his gut. Again. "Did you hear that?"

Twisting groans from grating metal made him cock his head. "I do now." He edged around me, jabbing a finger at the shelter entrance. "Circle around. Get downwind and stay there, understand?"

I jogged a wide circle around the buckling door, coming up behind it, straight in front of Shaw. I flipped him a thumbs-up, the extent of my sign vocabulary, then dropped onto my stomach in the grass. At least I didn't have to worry about a human scenting me. If I kept quiet and out of sight, I was golden. Except...the Richardsons had no qualms pitting fae against fae to protect their interests.

Muscles tensed along my spine. Why open the door we couldn't budge and risk making themselves vulnerable to attack? Was Shaw's spicy lure that powerful? Or was that exactly what they wanted us to believe? I didn't like this. It was too easy. They wouldn't surrender now, they had gone too far.

Frustration had me chewing on my lip. Too late for second-guesses.

Hinges squeaked and silver flashed as the door swung open. A blast of pressurized air tainted by urine, feces and stale blood hit me in the face, and I almost gagged. Fae, if I had to guess. Crawling nearer, I lined up with a part in the grass that let me keep an eye on Shaw.

The bottom dropped out of my stomach as a slender woman climbed the stairs on her hands and knees. Once her head cleared the doorway, she glanced over her shoulder, right at me, as if she knew I was there. Her pupils had swallowed her irises, leaving her eyes black voids. Her parted lips gave her the appearance of panting. In a blink, the moment ended and she resumed her crawl onto the ground.

Several yards away from the safety of the door stood Shaw, and the woman was ruining her pale gray pantsuit by crawling every inch of it to reach him. Her movements made my eyes twitch. I kept getting hung up on how her knees bent backward, like a giant grasshopper. I had trouble reconciling her insectoid scuttling with the curvy, middle-aged woman she otherwise appeared to be. Blonde hair whipped behind her head from the speed of her passing. Her otherness hypnotized me until I blinked.

Remember, you are the cavalry. Don't fall off your horse yet.

Those intense tendrils of fascination wrapping my mind cleared once I coaxed my gaze from the womanesque creature. All we needed was another lure-wielding fae on the playing field. What the hell was that thing?

Shaw watched her approach with a neutral expression, but panic welled behind my breastbone. He was out there standing that thing down alone. Screw the plan. I pushed up from my hiding spot as a jagged wire sliced into my throat. My skin sizzled where the rusted steel touched me. Barbed wire, really?

My back bowed as the person holding the garrote tugged to get my attention. I bit down on my tongue to keep from calling out for help. Shaw had his own problem barreling straight for him. I had to solve mine on my own or die trying.

"How many marshals did the conclave send us this time?" a man with a thick Texas twang asked over my shoulder.

"What you see—" I hissed, "—is what you get."

"I don't believe you." He tightened the strand, cutting into my throat. "You killed Ethel."

"Ethel?" I wheezed. "You named the worm Ethel?"

Metal shifted with the roll of his shoulders. "When in Texas…"

I gasped against the wire carving into my airway. "Who are you?"

"Forgive me, darlin'. Let me introduce myself," he drawled. "I'm Jake Richardson."

Black spots dotted my vision. If he was Jake then… "That thing out there is Bethany."

His laughter grated in my ears. "Beautiful, isn't she?"

His weight settled on me. He knelt over my legs, trapping them between his thighs.

Instinctive panic soured my stomach. His knees were close enough I could reach his kneecaps with my fingertips, but to do it I had to face plant and then swing my arm behind me. Without the support of my hands, my throat would cut into the wire seesawing toward my larynx. I wasn't sure if I could survive that kind of damage, let alone heal from it.

Anticipation spiked Richardson's scent as he tightened his noose and settled in to watch the show. He was salivating for the kill. Not my death, though that was coming, but Shaw's. I got the impression Richardson liked to watch. That didn't mean he wouldn't kill me in a blink.

Jealousy was a double-edged sword, and I swung it. "Your wife can't resist him."

He chuckled. "She isn't trying to."

Okay, maybe I was cutting in the wrong direction. "He will kill her."

"Not for long." He exerted slight pressure on the wire, eagerness shaking his hands.

I made a gurgling noise that managed to sound like disagreement.

"He can try. He might even succeed." Fingers tangled in my hair. "That's why I have you."

A snarl peeled my lips from my teeth.

He leaned down, scenting the skin under my ear. "You smell like…potential."

Inhales whistled through my nose. "Thanks…for the…compliment."

"You smell like power. Young. Fresh. Untapped." He groaned. "So raw, you might as well be human."

As far as insults went, that one missed the mark. Being human sounded nice right about now.

Shrill cries snapped my attention back to Shaw. The woman, Bethany, crouched in the grass in front of him. Red lines scored her white blouse. Claws were out and teeth were bared, but his hunger was absent.

Something sharp and hot like pride burned in my chest as he gestured her forward with the flex of his fingers.

"You care about him," my captor observed. "Are you more than partners?" Laughter shook him. "Of course you are. You're too young to know any better, and he's got you all figured out. It never ceases to amaze me that incubus, as a race, haven't gone extinct. All those women scorned..."

In hindsight, Shaw using his lure might not have been the best strategy. We had tipped our hand, and it gave them an edge.

Enraged screams filled the air as the woman sprang over Shaw's head, twisting in midair so her forearms raked down his spine. His back arched, a roar ripping from his chest. She settled into a fighting stance, her arms blocking her face. Sunlight hit the curved edges of the smoky blades embedded in a line down her elbows to her wrists.

My fingernails dug into the soft ground, the urge to run to Shaw overpowering. "You don't have to do this."

"Yes, I do," Richardson said softly. "It's do or die, and I plan on living."

Lack of oxygen made forming coherent thoughts impossible. The same weighted feeling hit me. *Balance the scales. Make him pay. His life for theirs.* "You killed all those fae."

"No," he sounded tired. "I saved myself."

"You only thought you did." Gritting my teeth, I let go. My face hit the ground, dirt went up my nose. Wire carved into the delicate skin of my throat, a line of fire that burned clear to my spine. Pain cut so deep, I forgot how to breathe. I wasn't sure I could, that my head wasn't ready to pop off my neck. Somehow I swung my torso left. That arm shot out, and my palm gripped his kneecap.

"What are you—?" His scream as I fed magic into him silenced the urges in my head.

Twisting onto my right side, I kept hold of his knee while shoving him off me. Keeping a tight leash on my powers caused my hands to tremble with strain. "What type of fae are you?"

"Half-bloods like you...have it all." His face contorted. "Fae power without...strings attached."

The man was insane. My life was a tangle of fae politics and obligations. Being a half-blood just meant I got sneered at whether I fulfilled my obligations or not. Full-bloods outclassed me. Oh yeah, and I had a twenty-five/seventy-five chance of being mortal. So yay! I might also get to die one day.

"You're spewing crazy." I upped the pulse of magic. "Tell me what I want to hear or this ends."

"I can't—" Blood coated his bared teeth. "It hurts too much."

Telling him I couldn't stop what I started would be counterproductive, but I did throttle back as much as I could.

"Answer me," I said, keeping my voice level, "and the pain stops."

A wild gleam lit his eyes as blood dribbled down his chin. "We ate them."

I blinked away my surprise at his abrupt change in topic. "What exactly did you eat?"

"All of them," he sneered. "We savored each one."

While my mind scrambled for traction, I hit on a possibility that made bile rise up my throat. "We found human blood at your wife's apartment." My hands felt dirty where they touched him. "Did you kill someone there?"

"A human? What would be the point? They are nothing. Less than nothing." His laughter sprayed his shirtfront—and me—with crimson spittle. "Though I wouldn't put it past that damned boggart. He never was quite right."

"Says the man confessing to eating mystery meat," I muttered.

"Fae, you stupid bitch," he snarled. "We eat fae."

Consumption of living fae tissue by humans to absorb residual fae powers... "You're *ghouls*?"

Ghouls got a half-page description in the academy handbook and a brief mention in class. No wonder the thought hadn't crossed my mind.

"We are *not* ghouls." He recoiled. "After we feast, we're as fae as you are."

"Not so much. I'm half fae regardless of my stomach contents."

His eyes narrowed.

"Wait." One last tidbit niggled at me. "If you were eating the fae, where does the taxidermy come in?"

"The acquisition of rare fae is an expensive habit." He stuck out his chin. "The art pieces subsidized that."

Art pieces. Art. Pieces.

I had no words.

None.

"You realize you can't eat fae until you become one any more than you can rub one on your skin to—? Never mind." In case this capture blew up in our faces, I didn't want to give him any ideas. "You're born fae or half fae or plain vanilla human." Fury glinted in his gaze, but the truth was the truth. "If you eat fae, their magic seeps into your blood. As it breaks down, it becomes toxic. Any effects—" such as sprouting freakish grasshopper legs, "—are short term. Human bodies aren't made to withstand the wear and tear. You can't sustain whatever powers you've stolen. You've been doing this for what—five years?" He stuck out his chin. "Your hourglass has to be running low on sand."

"The thing about sand…" he clamped a hand on my wrist, prying my grip from his knee, "…is there are more beaches where those grains came from. Yours, for example, is downright pristine."

Twisting my wrist, I formed an awkward handshake with him. "How is this possible?"

"Incubus." His gaze tagged Shaw. "It's what's for dinner."

Freaking monkeys. My control wasn't getting better. Richardson's resistance was. The effort wasn't draining me—he was.

"They were right, you know." He flipped me facedown into the dirt. "You are what you eat."

Cold fear solidified into an icy ball in my gut. Fighting him was like squaring off against Shaw. The more I fed him, the more powerful he became. Incubi digested the energy they consumed. I did too, sort of, but at a much slower rate. My rebound was days in coming. His was a few minutes, tops.

How to fight someone who could throw my best right back at me? I had to take him down like I would topple Shaw. But first I had to flip the power switch. I couldn't risk him getting any stronger.

Richardson gloated over me, twisting my arm parallel with my spine. The burst of pain amped up my magic, and he sipped it down on a sigh. *Not helping.*

I had to get myself under control. No more excuses, no more try. I had to do it.

I threw out my lifeline and lassoed memories of my mother. That crinkly thing her eyes did and the small twitch in her lips before she caved into guffawing laughter. The expression on her face the night I... *No*. Not that one. The strength of her arms wrapped around me as we waited for a conclave representative to arrive. Her promise to stand by me, to love me, no matter what happened.

And she did. I was all she had. If she lost me, then she had lost everything...for nothing.

Between one breath and the next, the white-hot burn of my power extinguished to a spark. Close enough. Flat on my face with an arm pinned behind my back, I had no leverage. I was stuck. Not my best plan. I had juiced him up, and now he was straddling my calves. At least he had ditched the garrote.

Bracing my right palm on the ground, I pushed up a few inches and allowed the weight of the barbed wire to yank itself free. Gulping unrestricted air, I shoved upward and threw all my strength into a reverse headbutt, smashing the back of my skull into his face. A satisfying crunch greeted me. His fingers vanished, giving me back the use of my left hand and allowing me to cock my right arm and throw it backward. My elbow connected with his ribs, and he wheezed over my shoulder.

Twisting hard to the right, I rolled us into the grass. I was digging my nails into the dirt when Richardson sprung at me. Lurching out of his reach, I got my feet under me and bolted toward Shaw.

"Thierry." His voice ripped from a throat gone raw.

For one terrible moment, my gaze locked with his. Blood dripped into his eyes from a gash across his forehead, but his fear was for me. Even as he deflected blows from his opponent, I was his main concern. My heart stopped, and I knew I couldn't lose him like this. Not to them.

The open door to the shelter gaped in the ground ahead. Unsure of the extent of the Richardsons' magical immunity, I ran down the stairs, inside their lair in search of an effective weapon to use against them. The smell hit me first, cold and bloody, like a freezer full of freshly butchered meat. A short hall gave me three options. I shot through the door on my right, where the cloying scent of death was weakest.

Footsteps thumped behind me. Richardson was on the stairs.

Inside a sterile white room, I flipped the door lock then ransacked the area, searching for a way to combat him.

"There are scalpels," a frail voice said, "under the counter."

"Who said…?" My hand flew to my mouth. "Oh my God."

"Yes," he chortled. "Pray to yours. Mine abandoned me long ago."

Behind a white curtain, strapped to a gurney, a slender male fought for his life. His skin was the color of a ripe avocado. His knees bent at odd angles beneath the sheets. He was nude except for the thin white sheet draped over his waist, covering him from the hips down.

Bile rose up the back of my throat when I saw his chest, sliced open, flaps of skin pinned to his sides, revealing organs pulsing as silver contraptions cradled them. Behind him, on the walls, were shelves filled with bespelled jars. In them, lungs expanded, hearts pulsated. All major organs were accounted for, and most were in pairs.

Fists pounded on the door. "Open this door."

"The scalpels," the male urged.

"Right." I headed for the counter and rifled through the bins underneath the first shelf. "Better than nothing."

"You're with the conclave?"

"I am." His voice brought my head up, and I forced what I hoped was a reassuring smile. "Marshal Thackeray at your service."

"Good." He relaxed against his paper-thin pillow. "Good."

The door rattled in its frame. Richardson was ramming it. Had to be. With a fistful of scalpels, I placed myself between the wounded fae and the monster about to barrel into the room pissed off and ready to brawl. Picking one blade from the others, I gripped it until my fingers went numb.

"May I?" the male asked.

I darted a glance back at him. He jerked his chin toward my handful of blades. "Uh, sure."

After so long being a victim, if a scalpel in his hand bolstered his courage, I owed him that.

He flexed the fingers of his nearest hand. "Cut the tether first, please."

I sawed through the thick nylon strap as the door burst open. After wrapping his hand around the stem of a blade, I turned to face Richardson. He braced in the doorway, face purple from strain. A faint musky odor perfumed the room, slithering over me, leaving chills in its wake. I shivered away the sensation.

Sweat droplets blossomed on his forehead. Maybe he had absorbed too much magic. Maybe his body was melting down and all I had to do was give him a firm shove toward No-Going-Backsville.

"His lure." The injured fae coughed. "He's using his lure."

I blinked at that. Either Richardson sucked at playing the seduction card, or hanging around Shaw had given me a degree of immunity from other incubus lures. Honestly, it was probably a little of both. Richardson wasn't attacking me, because he *thought* he already was. With his lure. Okay. This might work.

I let my shoulders slump. My arms fell limp at my sides, my grip on the scalpels sure. I widened my eyes the way I had seen Shaw's victims do dozens of times and shuffled toward Richardson. His face shone with perspiration. His victorious grin made me want to stab him there first, but I had other plans.

A sudden, keening cry bounced off the walls.

I hesitated, trying to get a reading off Richardson. Was his backup on the way? Did that mean Shaw was...? No. He couldn't be. While watching Richardson for a reaction, I continued playing the role of the lust-ridden zombie.

Wind rustled past my ear. My hand lifted on reflex at the same time Richardson let out a startled grunt. Blood coated my fingers. The tip of my ear was nicked, but a shiny silver handle stood out of his forehead. I whirled around, but the fae's head lolled. His unbound hand hung off the stretcher, his long fingers brushing the floor. A shrill beeping split my ears as his alarm cried for help and his monitor flatlined.

My vision blurred as I turned to face Richardson. He slumped on the ground, feeling around the wound, working up his nerve to grasp the handle and yank out the blade. He wasn't dead yet, and that told me he would heal from his injury. Probably thanks to me. Unless I put him out of commission first.

Before his fingers touched the warm metal, I grabbed the handle and yanked it out of his skull. I palmed his forehead, putting his skin into contact with as many of my runes as possible, and I let the trickle of power still lit from our earlier encounter flare to life with the heat of my anger.

Power left me in a rush. This time I didn't try to hold back, I didn't give him time to absorb the magic. No. This time I ruthlessly lit him up from the inside, until pale green light shone from his pores and his body seized.

Shaw was alone out there, and God only knew what other horrors awaited us down here.

Stoking the fires of my powers, I unleashed it all, burning through his veins as my magic sought out the spark of creation itself and clamped its jaws around Richardson's pathetic excuse for a soul.

Torn free with a squelching tug, a piece of rancid fruit plucked from a rotten tree, I devoured it.

Energy coated every inch of his skin. He was still twitching when I peeled away his flesh.

Kicking aside the husk of humanity left after Richardson's death, I jogged up the stairs. Too full of fear and magic to tap into common sense, I stepped onto the field without first checking for Shaw or the remaining Richardson. When fingers dug into the fleshy part of my shoulder, I clamped a hand around the thick wrist and, stepping into the body pressed flush to mine, sank my right elbow into…

"*Oof.*" Shaw hit the ground like a ton of bricks.

I fell to my knees at his side. "We have to stop meeting like this."

"Jake?" he mumbled.

"Dead." I took his hand. "Bethany?"

"Dead."

I hovered over him, afraid to touch him. One eye was reduced to a red, puffy slit. His bottom lip was split. The bottom third of his nose bent left. I traced the high edge of his cheekbone, the only part of his face not ruined. Being shirtless meant I got an eyeful of the carnage below his collarbone.

He winced when I touched the purple splotch blossoming under his eye.

I pulled my hand back despite his protests. "Do you want some help with this?"

"I'm good." He wet his lips. "I'll just— *Fuck.*"

My palm ignited. Energy arced between us, and instinct clocked Shaw's noble intentions upside the head. Poor guy had no choice, really. His hunger played moth to my flame, latching on and jolting me to the core. Tugging healing gulps of magic, Shaw drained the feeding buzz I was happy to relinquish.

I gave more than I should have, enough to erase Richardson's imprint, enough that when this case closed and I saw my bed again, I might get to sleep without his oily essence roiling in my belly.

"Thierry," Shaw groaned.

"Shh." I brushed damp hairs from his forehead. "I've got you."

CHAPTER SIXTEEN

I was sprawled on my bed at the dorm, ready to sleep for days, when my phone rang. Tempted as I was not to answer it, Shaw and I would be tangled up in paperwork and interviews for days, which meant not taking a call wasn't an option. I flicked the green icon and yawned. "Marshal Thackeray."

"You sound tired."

Shaw's voice in my ear made me smile. "Yeah, well, you sound exhausted."

He chuckled. "Did Mai finally go home?"

"About thirty minutes ago," I said. "I fell asleep when I was supposed to be admiring the flex of Jeremy Renner's biceps in some action flick she bought to add to her collection. Mai slapped me for insulting her man with my short attention span then left in a huff muttering about how I wasn't maid of honor material." I dug the remote from under me. "How about you? Are you home for the night?"

"Not yet." A bell tinkled in the background. "Did you call your mom?"

"She does not know and does not wish to know." If he heard the bitter edge in my voice, then he ignored it. He was polite like that. "If I get hurt on the job, I want her worst-case scenario to be some guy pulling a gun on me or a car accident or whatever else *CSI* has taught her kills cops. That's why I signed the cremation voucher my first day. Whatever happens, she doesn't need to know the truth."

His end of the call stayed quiet.

"Sorry." I swung my legs over the side of the bed. "I didn't mean to unload all over you."

"You're fine." Static crackled. "If I didn't want to know, I wouldn't have asked."

I screwed up the nerve to reciprocate. "What about you? Have you made your life-affirming calls?"

"I'm doing that now."

Heat swept through my chest, prickling up my neck. "Oh."

"Have you—?" A blaring car horn cut him short. "Asshole."

I scowled at the phone. "Excuse you?"

"Not you." He grunted. "Have you eaten?"

I covered my mouth, swallowing hard, forcing myself not to dwell on Tobias Long, the caelifera fae Mrs. Richardson had used as her food source for the last three months. "No. I'm not hungry. You?"

"Open your door," he answered.

"I'm in my pajamas," I warned him.

A teasing note entered his voice. "Same ones as last time?"

"No." I plucked at my Eeyore sleep shirt. "Unless…" I snorted, "…was that a request?"

"Sure," he said after a moment. "Take off the pajamas you're wearing."

Fingering the hem of my shirt, I walked around the room in search of Pooh. "And then?"

"And then open the door."

I straightened. "We're not at the place in our relationship where I answer the door nude."

A purely masculine groan vibrated in my ear. "Fine."

Knocking sounds commenced, and I cautiously approached the peephole in my door. What can I say? It had been that kind of day. Peering through the fisheye lens, I spotted a weary Shaw carrying a cardboard box with a familiar winery logo emblazoned on the side.

"What have you got there?" The words tumbled out before I got the door unlocked.

"Dinner." He slid past me into the room. Glass tinkled when the box hit the desk.

My eyebrows climbed. "Since when are you on a liquid diet?"

When his response was to mash his lips together, a sense of dread coiled around my chest. "Would you like ice or a glass with your meal?"

Shaw reached into the box and pulled out two bourbon glasses. "I've got us both covered."

I approached the desk and inspected a dark purple label on a wine bottle. "Sweet Dreams, huh?"

"Brewed by narcoleptic pixies under the full moon." He recited the label verbatim.

"Do we need—" I counted the corked tops, "—seven bottles?"

The thick-bottomed glasses hit the desk with a thump. "The evac team found the other shelters."

The cushion of wellbeing I had built up over the past few hours burst. "And?"

"The Richardsons sealed the vents over the four other containment areas the night before."

I dropped into the nearest chair, suddenly ready for that drink. "Were they occupied?"

"Thierry…"

Leaning forward, I braced my elbows on my knees and covered my face. "That's a yes."

"We couldn't have saved them," he said softly. "They were gone by the time we got there."

Biting the inside of my cheek, I nodded. "What about Mr. Long?"

"They couldn't save him." Shaw's hands settled my shoulders. "He died on the way to the medical ward."

"How do you do it?" I wiped the dampness from my cheeks.

He began a slow massage that made me feel worse for feeling better. "Believe it or not, sometimes the good guys actually win."

"Not this time."

"We stopped two people from processing fae like livestock. That's a win in my book."

"We don't know how they accessed those fae or how they transported them here. This happened in our territory.

We should have known." I gulped a sharp breath. "This doesn't feel like winning."

The firm hands on my shoulders vanished. "You have to take victories where you find them."

"Yeah" was the best answer I could manage.

"The magistrates reported the crime to the Faerie High Court. It's out of our hands." He circled until his boots touched my toes. "We caught the leak on our side. Now they get to plug the hole on theirs."

"How is that enough?" I examined the mud flaking from his boots onto the tops of my feet through my fingers. "For them or us?"

"It's all we've got." He sat on his haunches and pried my hands from my face. "The world is an awfully big place. You need to accept now that you can't fix it. Do the best you can to make it better when you leave than it was when you got here. That's all you can do. It's enough. It has to be."

Gazing into his eyes, witnessing his sincerity, made it easier shrugging off the guilt. For now.

"I also thought you might be interested to know the Richardsons' boggart has been taken into custody."

"I guess they had to remove him, huh?" He wouldn't allow the Richardsons' things to be collected and the apartment to be cleaned for listing otherwise. "He would have been one heck of a deterrent for potential renters."

"They removed him because evidence was found linking him to the disappearance of Rosalie Lindt." He explained, "She worked for a local maid service. She was the second Molly Maid to vanish after cleaning the Richardson's apartment."

The blood I found on the bed had been hers. "Thank you." I touched his cheek. "Her family deserves closure, even if they can't know her killer was captured."

Gaze dipping to the floor, he shrugged. "I was tying up a loose end in a case."

Knowing better than to press my luck, I pointed to the wine. "Are you pouring, or am I?"

"There's something I want to do first." He leaned forward, knees touching the ground. Walking forward on them, he wedged his hips between my thighs and wrapped his arms around my waist. Wide palms cupped my rear, dragging me closer until my hips were flush against his. "I almost lost you today."

I shuddered against him. "If I never see the inside of a giant worm again, it will be too soon."

"I'm serious." His hands glided up my sides, smoothed over my shoulders. His fingers trailed over my throat until he cradled my face between his warm palms. "You let that annuli swallow you."

"It was him or us." The math was simple. Even for me. "I chose us."

"This is me..." his warm lips brushed mine, "...choosing us."

I groaned into his mouth, hating to be the sensible one. "Are you sure?"

His face obscured my vision, his nose almost touching mine. "You don't trust me?"

I bit the inside of my cheek, but ultimately I told him exactly what had been bumping around in my head for the past few days. Sometimes I couldn't stop myself from blurting out the truth. "You're used to using the incubus thing as a shield. Someone wants sex, you lower the shield. Someone wants more than sex, you raise the shield and pump ten thousand volts through it to discourage climbing."

A crease formed between his eyes. "What?"

"Your dietary needs might be a restriction if I were, say, human. I'm not. I think I've proven that I can satisfy you." When the tiniest pinprick of white dotted his eye, I swallowed hard. "I meant that I'm capable of feeding you. The question is, can you survive on chicken-salad sandwiches night after night after night? Because dietary restrictions or not, if we do the dating thing, then I expect fidelity."

"In this analogy..." he rubbed his jaw, "...you're the chicken-salad sandwich?"

I nodded. "Correct."

"Then we have a problem," he said, withdrawing from me, his voice thick with regret.

The tense spot in my chest coiled tighter. "At least you're honest."

He used the arms of the chair to push to his feet. "See, I'm allergic to mayonnaise."

"You aren't serious." I hesitated when he reached for me. "Wait. Is the mayo thing an analogy for commitment?"

Without answering, he pulled me to my feet and spun me around, shoving me onto my bed.

"If only you were fried chicken." He palmed my shoulder and pushed until my back hit the mattress. "Or lemon chicken." He straddled my thighs. "Or even chicken tenders, then we could be together." Leaning forward, he covered my body with his much larger one. He braced a palm near my ear and bent down, letting me watch as his pupils faded to stark white. Nails on the hand beside me elongated, and he used them to slice through the fabric of my pajamas. "All this chicken talk is making me hungry."

I clutched the material over my breasts. "Too bad about your allergies."

"Tomorrow, after work." Shaw buried his face in my neck. "I'll pick up an EpiPen."

"Cute." I screwed my thumbs into his sides until his panting laughter made me chuckle.

Twisting to break away from me, he hit the edge of the tiny twin bed and tumbled onto the floor, bringing me down on top of him. I landed sprawled across his hips, which Shaw didn't seem to mind since he gripped mine and pressed down as his rolled upward against my core. My eyelids fluttered shut.

With reverent hands, Shaw slid my top down my arm, tossing it aside. I figured him for a breast man, but he just lay there, soaking in the view. "Beautiful." One leg hole in my shorts was intact even if the other side was cut down the seam. As he tugged the fabric aside, a rough growl vibrated through his chest. White rims circled his irises, but he was still Shaw, still with me. That primal, hungry part of him gazed out at me longingly, there one minute and gone the next.

Brushing his hands aside, I unbuckled his belt and popped the button on his jeans. His zipper tab was pinched between my fingers, his claws embedded in the carpet, when pounding started on my door.

A low snarl rose up his throat. "Ignore it." He gripped my hip hard enough to leave bruises.

Eyes crossing as he continued grinding against me, I slid the tab down one tortuous click at a time.

"Marshal Thackeray," a prim voice called. "I assure you ignoring us won't make us go away."

"Damn fae super hearing," I grumbled.

"We heard that," replied the slightly irked voice.

Shaw pushed up onto his elbows, leaning forward to capture my bottom lip between his teeth. The sound I made when he bit down earned me a throat-clearing through the door.

"I'm coming," I called. Shaw's husky chuckles made me flush ten shades of red. "*Shaw.*"

"Jackson," he corrected as he gripped my waist and lifted me onto my feet.

Unable to fit my mouth around his name, I scrambled over his long legs, hit the bathroom where I snagged a robe, then peeked through the hole in my door. A lean woman with pale blonde hair was checking her watch. Two men flanked her, both wearing black combat fatigues and carrying swords.

I gulped. "Um, Shaw, you might want to zip up for this."

Taking his time, he stood, fastened his pants and drew his shirt back over his head. He was well on his way to looking respectable by the time I opened the door and our guests entered my room.

"We have a lead on the poacher who supplied the Richardsons." The petite woman wrinkled her nose at the chair by the desk. One of her guards removed a packet of antibacterial wet wipes from his pocket and wiped down the seat. After the streaks dried, she sat. "Your magistrates were kind enough to offer your services to us in the hopes of apprehending them before they cross back into Faerie."

Shaw came to my side and folded his arms over his chest. "Who is *us* exactly?"

"My name is Irene Vause." Her laser-sharp glare would cut through steel like butter. "I'm a magistrate with the Northeastern Conclave."

I frowned at her. "An interdivisional loan?"

A dangerous edge entered Shaw's voice. "Why aren't your own people handling this?"

Her cornflower-blue gaze locked with mine. "We have our reasons."

"Thierry is a week into her OJT," Shaw said. "I'm not sure working outside our district is wise."

Another time, when I was less naked and more informed, I might have argued with him and his ideas for me. But he was my training officer, and my friend, and I trusted him to have a better reason for stepping between me and an opportunity than some misguided-caveman, almost-had-sex instinct.

"I am sure," Vause answered in a quiet voice. "We will double any bonuses you incur and cover all travel expenses." The edges of her lips twitched. "I understand you enjoy flying, Marshal Shaw."

I gritted my teeth in what I hoped passed for a smile. I knew that joyride would bite us on the ass one day, but I figured Mable or someone from accounting would be issuing the wrist slaps and not an actual magistrate. Considering I had only met our magistrates once in the five years I had been sheltered by them—on the night I was examined before being given sanctuary—I wasn't sure what protocol was in dealing with them. How hard could I push? How hard would they push back?

As if reading my mind, Vause asked, "What do you think of our proposal, Marshal Thackeray?"

I turned to my partner. "Shaw?"

"I asked for your opinion." Vause narrowed her eyes thoughtfully. "Not his."

Once again, the truth got the better of me. "I want the job."

"The money..." her gaze took in our surroundings, "...could improve your situation."

I took a step forward, and her guards did too. "I'm not in this for the money."

Amusement danced in her eyes, her expression softening. "Your father would be proud to hear you say so."

I set my jaw. "Paternal approval isn't a great motivator for me."

"Cash works for me," Shaw volunteered. "Not that anyone asked."

Vause raised a hand. The guard on her right placed an envelope on her palm. She then offered it to me.

"There are two first-class tickets to Wallagrass, Maine in there. Along with a few incidentals."

Tearing open the flap, I thumbed through the contents. Two tickets and a check for ten thousand dollars. Made out to me. "A few incidentals?" My fingers trembled. "This is a whole contingency plan."

"You have one hour." Vause held out her hand a second time. The guard on her left reached into his pocket, withdrawing a small object. The scent of strawberry lemonade filled the room as he popped the cap on a bottle of hand sanitizer. He squirted a generous amount into her palm, stopping at her nod. She stood while rubbing her hands together. "I expect a call when you land." She motioned to her guards. "You'll find my card in the envelope."

With a warning glance at me, the guard on the right ushered Vause into the hall. The guard who had been stationed on her left followed them out and shut the door on their heels with a gentle *snick*.

"From Wink, Texas to Wallagrass, Maine sounds like a long flight." Shaw hooked my robe with his finger and dragged me closer. "We should pack our own food. I hear what they serve on planes is terrible." His thumb absently stroked the lumpy knot in my belt. "What do you think?"

I bit my lip. "What are you in the mood for?"

His warm mouth closed over mine. "I never did get my chicken-salad sandwich."

AUTHOR'S NOTE

Dear Readers,

When I wrote *Heir of the Dog* as the first book in the Black Dog Trilogy, I planned Thierry's journey to span those three novels and no more. But then I attended the RT Booklovers Convention, and all that changed. *Heir* won the American Idol Contest, and that brought two agents with fresh ideas into the mix. The next thing I knew, the trilogy had expanded to include one more title – *Dog with a Bone.*

Dog with a Bone is a prequel to the series in the sense that the novella cuts a hole into the ceiling of Thierry's past and gives us a glimpse of those first steps that set the events of the trilogy into motion one year later.

With that in mind, I hope you have fun meeting Thierry as a bright-eyed cadet in *Dog with a Bone* and enjoy watching her mature through *Heir of the Dog, Lie Down with Dogs* and *Old Dog, New Tricks* into a woman who knows when laws should be upheld and when they are meant to be broken.

Best,

Hailey Edwards

ABOUT HAILEY EDWARDS

A cupcake enthusiast and funky sock lover possessed of an overactive imagination, Hailey lives in Alabama with her handcuff-carrying hubby, her fluty-tooting daughter and their herd of dachshunds.

Chat with Hailey on Facebook, **https://www.facebook.com/authorhaileyedwards** or Twitter, **https://twitter.com/HaileyEdwards**, or swing by her website **http://haileyedwards.net/**

Sign up for her newsletter to receive updates on new releases, contests and other nifty happenings.

She loves to hear from readers. Drop her a line at **http://haileyedwards.wufoo.com/forms/contact/**

HAILEY'S BACKLIST

Araneae Nation

A Heart of Ice #.5
A Hint of Frost #1
A Feast of Souls #2
A Cast of Shadows #2.5
A Time of Dying #3
A Kiss of Venom #3.5
A Breath of Winter #4
A Veil of Secrets #5

Daughters of Askara

Everlong #1
Evermine #2
Eversworn #3

Black Dog

Dog with a Bone #1
Heir of the Dog #2
Lie Down with Dogs #3
Old Dog, New Tricks #4

Wicked Kin

Soul Weaver #1

Made in the USA
Middletown, DE
11 September 2019